passages

Books by Ann Quin

Berg
Three
Passages
Tripticks

ann quin
passages

DALKEY ARCHIVE PRESS

Originally published in Great Britain by Calder & Boyars Ltd., 1969
Copyright © 1969 by Ann Quin

First U.S. Edition, 2003

Library of Congress Cataloging-in-Publication Data

Quin, Ann, 1936-1973.
    Passages / Ann Quin.—1st U.S. ed.
       p. cm.
    ISBN 1-56478-279-4 (pbk. : alk. paper)
     1. Brothers and Sisters—Fiction. 2. Schizophrenics—Fiction. I. Title.

PR6067.U5 P37 2003
823'.914—dc21

                             2002073508

Partially funded by grants from the Lannan Foundation and the Illinois Arts Council, a state agency.

Dalkey Archive Press books are published by the Center for Book Culture, a nonprofit organization with offices in Chicago and Normal, Illinois.

www.centerforbookculture.org

Printed on permanent/durable acid-free paper and bound in the United States of America.

NOT that I've dismissed the possibility my brother is dead. We have discussed what is possible, what is not. They say there's every chance. No chance at all. Over a thousand displaced persons in these parts, perhaps more. So we move on. Towards. Away. Claiming another to take his place, as I place him in profile. Shapes suiting my fancy. Rooms with or without connecting doors. He watches when she isn't around. A perverse protection he knows she needs. From his need

he takes notes. For a book. Journal. Report in some hotel. I no longer question. Parts of him I want to know, others he tells me of. Trips he has made here before. The sea. Fruit. Dry river beds. Beds slept in, not slept in. Back, from islands. Concrete islands. Barren. Cultivated. Sunlight before the rain. Violence of day by day these thoughts. Stirs fingers onto insects at night. Their mark on white walls. Her head rolling in afternoon sleep. As in the half dark room, he listened to music. I listened to sounds, waited for those that never came. I didn't look up. Their bodies rotated, she above. Legs, arms moved with the music over him. On the floor, the bed. They made a tent of the sheet. Light in parts of skin. Movement so near, by stretching my hand into the open

I heard cicadas, wind colliding with trees. Sounding an ocean in the long room. I opened the shutters. Town huddled above the sea. Thin shadows of cypresses. She stood over him, he pushed her down onto her knees. I drew the curtains. I couldn't see, but saw what next would happen. I was thirsty. Water heavy with smoke, heat, a bitter taste. Hardness of the glass, she saw herself in. Buzz buzz buzzing of a mosquito round a candle. Wax formed green rivers. Frozen. I tried lifting him from the floor. Laughter. Afterwards recognised as my own. The sea a faint white line. A longing

for rain. Olives dried in the sun no longer sensations. Grapes whiter from dust, sand, shaken in water. Seaweed he put round the bed, when my hair, neck were no longer part of the seaweed. Sun behind rocks. Shadow columns from fig trees, where I slept. Woke up hanging over the bed. In the next room I pictured her smile, larger it seemed than the face could hold. She held his head. He in a praying position, about to throw up. He moved between mirrors, measured the two rooms. Appeared naked on the balcony. Ah here you are I wondered where you had got to. He turned away, murmuring. Heat so unbearable if only it wasn't so dry if only it would rain. He gestured as if opening the sky. Split in half. He turned the air conditioner up.

We drank small cups of black coffee, thick, sweet. And sucked halva. Bread from an oven, in another part of the house. A spiral stairway he went down. She looked in the round mirror. Walls of mirrors. Circles of water, trees, faces edged off by shifting light. He rubbed an oblong stone. A fig opened slowly. Lips thin. Eyes narrowed on the deeper textures. Moments flashed, yellow, blue, orange. Sky so blue startles the eyes. Lying down I no longer saw the sea. Land a desert. Gulls, paper-wet, screamed. She looked for her brother against marble, steel railings, entrance halls, hotels. A museum I remember where I came across his signature, that perhaps wasn't there at all.

Up from the beach we held hands, ran across the dunes.

6

The lower dunes where we lay. Tall grass sand shaken, surrounded. Oceans of sand swallowed up crevices. The beach long, narrow. Hollows, patches, marks where others had been buried. Underwater we circled fish, each other. Shadows grew, slid across, terraced. Making patterns she leaned from. Hills of sand our shadows slipped over. We ate grapes dipped in the sea, salt added to their sweetness. Taken out of their skins. Wasps settled on the remains. Shoal of small white fish unchained at the water's edge. His hands cupped under. Network of fingers over the sea. Waves recoiled from places they struck. Hands felt the dry under parts of sand. One hill

in darkness. Sheep, goat bells heavier as we approached. Town lights, a fallen nest of fireflies, between the hills. Groups of musicians outside cafes. Men played dice. We were strangers. We were accepted, ignored. Initial curiosity. They went back to their beads, dice, drink. Men danced with men. Women watched, pretended not to. Priests still walking in cemeteries, passed by smiling, hands raised, gathered more dust on their robes, beards. Older men carried on gambling, talked of the political situation, fishing, money, the war. Countries they had seen, not seen, hoped for their sons to see. They spoke at times in a dialect we didn't understand. We were misinterpreted. Information given in exchange for money, clothes, cigarettes, drink. We were misinformed. He has now understood we have no choice, so we move from hotel to taxi, from taxi to train. Dining car to sleeper.

Blinds half way. Dips of black, quarter whiteness. Patches of water along the coast. Rain walked designing its own shadow. Winds condensed on summits, the straight sides of mountains. The sea cut swift movements of clouds. Over valleys grown wider, deeper, where rivers continually change their position. Bases of the hills bent back towards the course of the river. Lights, signs from cities, villages, towns I know only from maps, brochures. Long empty stations. Tracks

7

criss-crossed. A man walked along, swung a red light. Silence of the train halt. Shadow thrown on a long wall. He must have stood by the window. I slid the doors open. He wasn't there. The train moved on, stopped, hissed, shuddered. Form of horses

gathered, tossed their heads. Neighing grew fainter. Sound of hoofs on dry earth. Marble and limestone. Movement of not seeing her, perhaps dust blinded. I thought I heard his voice from another compartment. She stood in the doorway. He didn't look up. He used a new pen. Creases around his mouth, eyes. Creases in trousers. Hand groped for the table. He fell forward. The whisky bottle empty. Day after day, the nights slid across, rolled under. Windows closed. What's the time then? He twisted her wrist round. Your watch has stopped must have stopped. Hands pulled blinds up, down. On shutters, between them, lifting one slat up. Fingers in hair, the spine, scratches marked the outline of ribs. Note-paper covered in illegible writing. He works out a route, statement, report. His hand covered the paper, screwed it up, thrown out of the window, under the train. He drew slowly on the cigar, eyes half closed. Hands rested between his legs, head bent back, fingers sprang out, moved as though emphasising some dialogue.

We went for a drink. Another part of the train. A fat priest opposite a nun. Crucifix swung against hair, beard, chest, hair. The nun rose in the folds of blue light. We sat at the bar, avoided looking in the mirror opposite. He glanced occasionally sideways. A circle of wetness on polished wood she made many circles from. Swift turns his head made. She knew it was impossible. She remained. The drink became warm water. His knuckles red, dark hairs slipped through. I felt their weight. The heavier parts of window frames, wheels, metal. I leaned nearer. His head struck his arms. Out of trees her laughter came, went. The corridor twisted from me.

8

Doors rattled open, closed. Shapes darker closed in. A passing line of birds. In the dust, a sudden stirring of wings, out of branches.

He lay on dry leaves, a strand of yellow grass in his mouth. A large nest abandoned, her fingers traced the fibres, the rough surface of grass and twigs. He stood up, rose on his toes, chest thrust out, his head tossed back, forward. Women passed, water jugs on their heads. A place he knew, brought her to. He spoke of other places, women he'd known, wanted to know. I laughed, danced round him. He never dances. His hands feel the table's length. The hardness of that. Smoothness. Knees under moved together, separated. Rings up and down her fingers. Along earth wrinkles. The white of his eyes before completely shut. Shape of mouth corners shapes the corners of his eyes. Eyebrows. The shape of thoughts. Dreams

between tall buildings. Drone of traffic. He listened for the key to turn. Steps in carpeted places. Dialogue. What to say, what is anticipated, what is not. Accusations. Apologetic her smile. He gave his High Priest look from his Zen position in the middle of the bed. Submission to the image. To departures he perhaps sees from the hotel, through shutter slits. As she kisses her escort from the night. Perhaps a little curiosity. Double bed not slept in. The extra one with blankets in a heap. Notepaper on desk. Briefcase shiny brown. His shoes, less shiny, neatly together under the desk. Rooms we take the shape of. Yellow, white light crept in, when it could be any time of day. When she makes love with men younger than herself. Number amongst numbers. Room 311. He unfolded from his stunted position, and took out the ear plugs, their small roundness in his arm pits for softening. Shaped to his ears. The shape of these she came back to. Hello had a good rest? I think his eyes were open. He didn't reply in the darkness

9

of the compartment. Light held a soft yellow lump in its blueness. His words weighed, as he bent, picked up a cigarette. A pebble. He slung the pebble out to sea. I thought he was shaking, but it was the lurch of the train. We'll be there on time—we'll make enquiries once we get settled in. I remained in an upright position, and saw her body unfold from the folds of her dress. Motions of undressing alone, the quickness. And when with someone. Hair brushed slowly. A face behind the face.

Faces of officials. My own for them. No I don't belong to the Party, my brother might have done—I don't know. We were followed. We knew they were there in hotel lobbies, restaurants, cinemas, parks, cafes. Quite by accident I am involved. The cab driver watched us in the rear mirror. To be on the move again at least is something, he said, looking out of the back window. Whiteness of buildings at the checkpoint we were not allowed to cross. Perhaps they think we are spies, he said, laughing, and caught hold of her bracelet. Maybe we can bribe them.

Our papers were apparently not in order. The men played cards, smoked, coughed and spat under the unshaded light. The interpreter was expected in the morning. He arrived at noon, a small fat dog under his arm. His hands dug into the dog when I offered him the money. The dog watched us. Complexities of ringed fingers came up through the dog's wiry hair. Shutters closed around us. Silence outside. The guard made advances. Curly hair, sensual mouth, a girlish face. He continually slapped at flies. In another room a babble of voices, scrape of chairs. Paper rustled, numerous papers, forms we were told to fill in. Sweat trickled from the interpreter's forehead, above his mouth, through his moustache. There is one paper missing, he said, and offered me a cigarette, which I refused. We went to a longer, narrower room. The fan was out of order. A button had fallen off the interpreter's

10

shirt. Glint of cross, medal. I continued playing the part, I had no alternative after the money had been refused. She could tell how late it was by the barking of dogs, persistent, from one to another, across the town. His steps above, one two one. Two. One two. A scar on the interpreter's hand, thin purple on white, under the black. He panted. The dog whined from the table. Does God laugh at Himself madam— ah I beg your pardon you are a non-believer I notice from your papers. He laughed, edge of teeth over lower lip, made sucking noises, made as though he looked at the dog. Coiled his fingers round its collar. He offered me some melon. It's a pity I have a weak heart madam my dog has a weak bladder we make a good pair don't you think? Pool on the table trickled over some flowers. The dog sat on its haunches, lay on its back, pawed the interpreter's arms. I could not see the interpreter's eyes. A dozen lights spun in his spectacles. Two ringed plump fingers round the phone. Ah good your missing papers have been found—I hope you have a pleasant journey madam and good luck—God be with you—ah forgive us for the slight misunderstanding—a case of mistaken identity let's say. He half bowed. We shook hands.

Bundle of chickens, tied together by their legs, fluttered on the stairs. He sat on a bench, reading a newspaper. Pages he cut open with the edge of his hand. Finally he folded it together, creased on the inside, straightened out on the outside, and smoothed the surfaces. We were waved through the Control, men half drunk, asleep. She had seaweed in her hair, pieces of melon skin round her nails. The interpreter stood at the window, his face buried in the dog.

Land crusts. Staircases round a tower. Black flights of steps. Paper flowers, beer cans, wine bottles surrounded small white crosses. Unmade roads curled above chasms. Sea left behind, interior of mountains yawned in all its ridges, furrows, and closed up. Clusters of white buildings, olive trees, cypresses.

11

Half naked children squatted outside broken gates, doors, fences. Then he exploded, they have no right to keep us that long—interrogate us like that. Men looked vaguely up from cafe tables. Old, young women in black, took washing in, bent over ovens. Buildings turned pale yellow. Wind came off the sea. Spray on the pavements, roads, mixed with dust. God I think we're still being followed, he whispered, what is it they want?

The train halted. From his compartment it was day. From mine I saw the stars, glimpse of water, my face landscaped. Hairline around the mouth. Trees. The train moved on. Long front part twisted into, out of tunnels. He slid the doors apart, swayed there, grinning. Does he laugh at himself when alone? Eyes blink when dreaming. What are his dreams, needs, obsessions, demands, desires. Fantasies he rarely shares? The strangling of the interpreter's dog with its collar.

We'll soon arrive I've spoken to the porter. He flexed his wrist. Smudge of egg at the mouth corners. Sun squeezed between mountains. Mountains met clouds, many islands. A city he knows, that might be any city. A square, fountain, skyscrapers, blocks of concrete, steel, crystal towers. Cafes, dark humid interiors, waiters straightened up, weaved between potted plants. She stumbled over cripples in alleys, passage ways, knew they heard the rattle in her throat. The thought of knives thrown at her back, bent over the bill. Waiting. She knew this role well. Beggars played theirs to everyone's embarrassment. The dull thud of a body pushed out by the manager. She looked at the newspaper. Surrounded by ashtrays, bottles not quite empty. By the sea, even there eyes evaded, knowing he watched as she searched shapes appearing, crawling towards her, amongst his clothes, on chairs, the floor. Once she was dressed, he no longer wanted the day. His face pushed into two pillows, under the blankets, felt the pressure of her hands

12

his that traced, retraced his background. Personal, public, racial connotations. Treks across deserts. Impressions filled in, covered by other flights. Other directions. Lack of water, the promise of. Veins of dry blood, veins shifted with shapes. Taste of bread, smells of synagogues. Sperm. The drying of that between pyramids, she pressed together. His hands, their feet, moved forward, back again over her. The incinerators would come later. She waited. In the waiting he drew his fingers out. Spread in front was the route they'd take. A route he knew well. She saw it from below. Above. In a downward movement her body stiffened, recognised the area between would be space soon enough. She heard the wind tear at steel. Guns, engines controlled the screams. Line of men against the wall, blindfolded, they fell forward, sideways, back. Gun metal revolved in particles of light. Puffs of smoke. The burnt flesh around those waiting in dark places that had no air. Grille held the hand. Her fingers slid over tongue through black bars.

He clicked the lighter, attention held by the flame. Sparks of light behind closed eyes. We'll arrive on schedule the headwaiter has told me. He suppressed a yawn, swallowed. Adjusted his tie, ordered some more coffee. I know of a good hotel we'll book in there for a night perhaps a couple of nights see how things go. Landscape formed the angle of her head. Buildings jutted out of rocks, above the sea. A sea changeable in colour, circulation from one moment

to the next. One face amongst thousands. Somewhere. Steps white, whiter than curtains limply out of windows. People bundled out of the train, were met. Not met under grey arches where pigeons had their nests. City outskirts. The centre, the main street located, as always. Into that, under narrow sky margins. Thin dust on roads, pavements. We climbed out of the cab. A man wearing a seersucker suit, straw hat with scarlet band, stood in a doorway. I thought I recognised him.

I could not be sure. He kept his hands in his pockets. We caught another cab, made a detour of the city, and booked in at a smaller hotel.

Large bed faced the square ornate mirror. How long are they going to keep it up, he shouted. I changed into another dress. He sat up, sank back, groaned. Be careful while you're out—I mean on your own you never know—will you be late again?

She moved past headlights, neon signs, quickly. A city she wanted to explore. It proved difficult. She let herself be picked up. A nightclub where she danced. No communication except by gestures. Laughing, the boy ordered more wine. Soon he indicated a drive by the sea. His body a lighter brown as he leaped the waves. She didn't look at his eyes. Darkness made this easy. Easier for falling together. Making a wetness tasting of salt, lemons, and almonds. I listened to the breakers, dug my heels into the sand, into the impressions he made beside me, under me. Lights from fishing boats, pernod colour, hung in space. Motors turned off. Shape of distant islands reared, knelt, rose again. Humps, shoulders of land turned over. The bite in her neck, he would remark on later, with a smile. Biting into melon. We slept beside an upturned boat. From a dream startled I thought for a moment he was someone else.

He sat up, scratched his head, chest, shook off sand, and ran towards some rocks. I waited for him to turn. He jumped, danced a crazy dance, surprising some gulls from a carcass. I scrambled up the bank. At the top I put my sandals on, turned and shouted out. He did not hear. Or look round. I caught the first bus back to the south section of the city. Roofs half in shadow. Trees towards the centre dark, edges light. My dress stained with wine and the sea. Sand fell in the hotel. Lift. The corridor.

14

He was in the same position as she had left him. Though she knew he must have rolled, turned many times in the night. I held the shell and fell asleep. Sleep entered the afternoon. He jerked the blinds up suddenly, and bent over the bed. Smell of disinfectant, hair tonic, after shave lotion. Bald patch at the back of his head, he rubbed when impatient, excited, tired. I turned over, mouth found the shell, the curvatures still tasting of the sea. He sat at the desk, scarlet dressing gown wrapped into body folds. In the shower I turned the taps off. I thought I heard him on the phone. A praying mantis climbed the window. Only glass, the coolness of that touched. The mantis motionless, its underside wrinkled, phylloid. Forelimbs clasped something that twitched. Water ran over my shoulders, neck, back. Pressed against the wall, hands slipped down. His climbed up above my head, clasped the sides. She fell forward, laughing under

trees, in gardens where statues were arranged in shaded areas. Fountains no longer in use. Wild flowers out of stonework. Shadows stretched over the terrace, from there met the steps, where he froze, one hand on his heart, the other pointed at a procession of nuns. I couldn't see their faces. Hands plucked at their habits, rosaries. He waved, ran down the steps. He held a bunch of artificial flowers, brightly coloured, sprayed with heavy perfume. I dropped one by one along paths of dry leaves. Somewhere the sound of a brass band. A waltz, a march, an overture. Wagner, he said. Plastic swans floated in an artificial lake, bobbed up, down, near the edge, where families picnicked. Screams of those from the funfair. Screams of countless machines rocked, shot, spun bodies that writhed in space, sudden, short. Gravity anticipated, shuddered at when touched. And laughter that laughed because it was expected.

High above a temple illuminated. The nuns paused, heads bowed over guide books. Beggars shouted from crouched positions. Legs, half legs curled under arms. Some had hands, but no feet. Some had legs, but no arms. They could not be ignored, though their faces were part of the wall they leaned against. Further down on a strip of beach, people packed under sunshades. Smell of fish just caught, rope, tar, drink. His hands round the glass, veins pressed under hairs, lighter from cuffs to knuckles. Hands above his head, marking the design of some unfamiliar birds. Slant of wings to the slant of their bodies under, caught the light falling. They turned from a straight course into a curved one, remained at the same height, wings on the convex side of their curving movements, moved in line. Lines

under his eyes, mouth. His mouth betrayed the eyes' attention on the play we saw that night. Actors in masks. I couldn't distinguish them at the party afterwards, held at a large villa overlooking the sea. The actors still wore their costumes, later exchanged, thrown off, as they danced in the gardens. On carpeted lawns. Played guitars in a boat to the nearest island. Streamers, fireworks flung across water. Three forms of shadow, columns without end, pyramid shaped, larger in receding, and pyramids that terminated as we reached shore. Flowers crushed on bodies. Their print underfoot. Formations in the formation of waves in sand, later lifted by a south by south east wind.

We dragged the boat up between plane trees, open spaces within, the circumference lost, only those at the sides remained. Tropical plants, rubber ones, illuminated. A fountain spurted coloured water. We climbed the stairs. Hi-fi music filled the courtyard. Someone picked up a dead rat. A woman screamed. Another woman, naked under arcs of blue, bounced her breasts. I went from room

to empty room. Large halls. Ceilings decorated with chariots, cherubs, centaurs, gods, goddesses. A Pan-like figure held the sides of a concave mirror. Grinning he glided across,

16

finger on mouth. He opened doors, windows. Walls divided by sky. The sea. Lights from the mainland. He was swept away by a group of musicians. From a certain angle he looked yes he looked like

I ran on, knowing I was being followed. She came to the edge, jumped into expanding blueness, ultra violet tilted as she went towards the beach. We walked in silence. Half cylindrical waves kept their direction when intersecting. Movements of the water's impressions penetrated each other, without changing their first shape. Sand settled in a square ridge on the steep bank. Music faint. Fainter as we walked another stretch of beach. We sat, smoked, drank some wine. He later threw the bottle against rocks. Fragments of green glass fell in the pool, amongst oysters feeding on the animal-culae. She left him, his head dangled over the rock. His body half buried by sand. Flowers and bones, burnt out fireworks, shrivelled balloons, shells, broken glass, ash in the water, she stepped out of.

Into the swimmingpool. Rubber rings, branches, fruit skins bumped the sides. White wall surround, where Siamese cats stalked, raised their pale fawn faces, narrow, to a narrower moon, and howled. Other unseen creatures answered. Roosters crowed, that crow all day, and nights of the full moon, when oysters fully open. Peacocks strutted under arches, cried their cat-like cries, made abrupt flights from each to each other. Through tall grass, unswept by the wind, but flattened in places by span of feathers. Movements of air nearest resembled movement of their wings pressed on it. Our bodies not touched, except by accident. Mountain rocks reddish, parts in light fawn-coloured. Branches contained shadows of every other branch, the light on one side extended equalled the shadow's shape. From here

he stretched up, touched the fruit, branches, until the fruit fell into shade, where he bent. The sweetest are those pecked

17

by birds here see. He held the small roundness out, between thumb and finger. Held in his mouth, half eaten, warm. Juice ran down finger sides. Below the valleys stretched towards the sea, wide, where rivers had widened, worn away the mountain roots along their sides. Window edges held two different lights, framed the sea, met the horizon. Areas he attempted filling in. Cigarette, drink, is there an ashtray anywhere? Eyes turned, sidelong, back again. Fingers on fruit, wood, material, cup, glass. Aspects of light thrown from each object. Spaces between

arms, legs. He stood against the window, swayed in a direction his head turned from. She watched some birds in rapid flight over the sea. Fruit squashed on the path, surrounding stonework, where insects gathered. The mountains, where once fishes moved in large shoals. Downward outline of the hills, bases of the mountains closer together. He picked up lemons, held against his face, scattered at my feet. Contained in their odour. Blue flowers lost their blueness in a room caught between two others, but gave back their colour in the glass. Journeys made there, through spherical shapes. Shaped in the moving lines of light. That side of his face patterned, continually interchanged, contradicted the turns he made towards the centre of the room. Centres of flowers. Pine cones. Lemon skin in his hands. Coolness of air rushed in the ear. I heard distinctly the sea, until he dropped the shell between us. It split in half. Grains, sand grains of varied length spread, took on the colour of what was in the room. Objects he touched, ran his finger along. Blue dust, pollen he rubbed off. One hand

up against the sun. We walked through the valley, along a river bank. A harvest festival held, where no river no longer ran into the sea. In a sudden sweep of wind through the valley, singing men and women. Trees bent in the wind's direction, circles of dust on the threshing floor, filled with swaying bodies. Sand rose in the distance, spiralled against banks of sand, merged, cutting into vineyards, harvest fields. Women paused, black against yellow, faces hidden in scarves. Horses raised their heads from watering. Harvesters stooped, gathered in what had been scattered. Trees bent in the opposite direction, and birds no longer beat their wings in oar strokes. He walked ahead, stopped, pointed at something on the ground. A snake moved over, up across a rock, disappeared in the undergrowth. We climbed the bank, slipped in ruts, mule tracks, but made no tracks of our own.

Couples strolled, paused, quickened their pace towards the church. Entered archways, cracked grey, white. Towards the doorway, lit by coloured lights, candles. Bony fingers made the sign of the cross. Mouths prepared for kissing the mummified saint. She straightened up from a kneeling position, one knee still bent, her shoulders shook. The priest's cloister paleness paler in that light. Death is not to be regretted my child so let us pray—many have died in this country—many have been buried unidentified—but let us hope—let us pray to the Almighty that

From icons, statues of saints dressed in tinsel, sequins. From their smiling painted faces, into that side of the shaded street people walked quickly up steps, into, out of large buildings. Buses churned up dust, sand. Neon signs, day and night, red, yellow, blue. Orange light twitched on the hotel walls from a sign opposite. He lay smoking. Dark spokes of the fan across his face. Angle of his body met the angles of her arms, legs. The shape of these shaped her moods. Fingers along ridges, furrows. She locked her legs and arms around. His hand under her left armpit. He held the bunch of fruit, dropped one by one into her mouth. She drank some wine, held in, onto him, and held him there. His head raised, eyes closed, under

the stream of water. An eagle motionless above. I heard the rush of wings. A low cry of some smaller animal. Grass

19

disturbed by grasshoppers that bounced over, through, at times not distinguishable from the grass. They sprang in all directions, as we walked towards the track, round the hill. Mountains on one side. Sea below where we sailed in the shadow of an island. Dolphins leaped one behind the other, behind the package boat that stopped off at many islands. Unloaded, loaded cargo, mail, families. Bundles of black shrouded women carried large baskets, chickens, babies. The men nursed melons.

An island, volcanic, we had been told of. A few fishermen worked the closer shore. Houses half in ruins. Small birds fluttered between shafts, grape vines. Trees unpruned. Between the darker blue a glimpse of sky. Gap in the wall held part of the sea. We walked uphill to the graves, many had fallen apart. Faint writing on weathered stone. Clouds, trees displayed no roundness in their shadows, where graves piled up, spread beyond broken railings, mounds, rocks perhaps once graves. The sea no longer visible as we climbed further up. Caves of branches he parted. Goats leaped over rocks. An old woman sat in the shade, brought out bread and fruit. A man beside her, his arms cut off at the elbows. I'll be your guide, he said, grinning. Broken black teeth, one side of his face scarred, one eye hung down, met his cheek covered with black hairs. He offered us some bread, wine warmed by the sun. I'll show you around this island. His stumps winged the space between the old woman, the food. Sit down sit here. A cigarette held between his patterned joints. Ah the war killed off many of us see what it did to me. The woman clicked her remaining teeth, nodded, broke the bread. I saved up and went abroad for artificial arms but they hurt so I do without—my sister has not enough money for a dowry so she remains unmarried—I too would like to marry—ah so it is—but life is good eh—come I will show you where we can swim without the sharks getting us.

A small inlet, the sea quieter green. Trees bent under their heavy load of figs. She felt his stumps round her neck in the water, further down, rubbing, two animals nuzzled her elbows, neck, and in between. She laughed, and struggled away. We walked in single file along a ridge, into the village. Fish flapped on cobbles, but firmly meshed in a net. A man held an eel, swung it down several times, the blood spattered, spread out under his feet. Heat from ovens through doorways. The smell of bread. The chief of police sprawled across the table.

A house consisting of four rooms. Grapes around, over the patio. You can rest here there's no boat anyway until tomorrow or the next day—it is nice here we make you comfortable plenty of food drink—yes rest here. A room dimly lit. Candles, icons, statue of the Virgin with brightly painted face, looked down from an alcove above the bed. His sister, dyed red hair, bent over, giggled, whispered, touched my clothes, hair, rings. Texture of skin soft where her black clothing parted. I heard laughter in the next room. Sound of mosquitoes. Pale light on the walls. His shadow grew, broke up the icons. Someone sang outside. A face at the window. Music entered the house. The entry slow, rhythm increased. Heat of my body slipped into my head. Waves of light behind the eyes. Behind his head. He lay on his side. He turned over. His arms fluttered, shadow of these in the other room.

We slipped out to the harbour at sunrise, and bribed a fisherman to take us back to the mainland. Six hours under cloudless sky, unstirred water changed from green, pale, darker blue. Fish shadows amongst the underwater vegetation. The fisherman at the tiller, he moved with one hand, hardly at all. The boat steered a straight course. His other hand continually passed over his brow, neck. His eyes riveted on us. Once he looked away, pointed at a barren island. There they took six men and shot them—tied rocks to their feet and threw their bodies into the water—no one ever recovered them—good food for the sharks eh. He pushed down his straw hat, faded, whiter than the foam on the sand edges of the island. Seaweed covered rocks. Blackish fronds coiled across parched grass. We skirted the shadow of this island, another loomed ahead. A small chapel perched on the top-most rocks, gulls flew onto, away. Then down, crying, dived headlong into the trail of the boat. I trailed my fingers down the side, into, along the water. Coolness of that on my neck. His. The motor turned off as we approached land.

The harbour deserted, shutters down. We couldn't find a cab. We went into a cafe. A woman with gold teeth behind the bar. She watched us, every move, gesture. He watched her, the way she swayed from the waist, hips, as she moved from bar to table. I went out

along the deserted street. A market, stalls laden with fruit, vegetables. Behind these men smoked, slept. Hunks, bodies of meat swung from hooks under dozens of naked bulbs. Meat on a spittal flies crawled over, into. Pigs' heads grinned above the mens' bowed heads. The sky slits through iron girding. Behind the stalls, vans, wooden boxes, crates piled up to the arch of iron, steel. Cries of animals waiting in the slaughter yard. I picked up a cantaloupe from under a barrow. The yellow of that in my hands, the curved lines.

I walked in shade, where possible, up a hill. And rested on a bench overlooking the harbour. The sun passed its meridian point. Signs of activity showed in the small groups of sailors, fishermen walked slowly towards boats. Men in door-ways, rubbed their eyes made kicking gestures at dogs. Arranged, rearranged tables, chairs. Shutters flung open. Sound of engines started up.

Shouts, laughter as she reached the main street. Whistles,

more laughter. I couldn't locate the cafe. I made enquiries. A group of men surrounded me, gesticulating. The woman swept the steps. The place was empty. I questioned her, she didn't understand. She chuckled, gold teeth flashed, eyes rolled. She went back to sweeping. Black stockings with holes, ended where her thighs began, brown skin supple. Her loose breasts swung in motion to her measured sweeps. She leaned on the broom, squinted at the sky, her hand rubbed the sides of her dress, a wet patch in front. I caught a cab back to the hotel.

Sounds from the radio. Air conditioner. He rubbed the stubble on his jaw. We've been invited to dinner by one of those actors I don't feel like making it why don't you go I may join you later. He didn't look round as he spoke. Odour of the cafe, fish, wine, old clothes, perfume from his shirt on the bed. Rings under the sleeves. His hand moved from one edge of the paper to the other. But his head so tilted his eyes were elsewhere. Perhaps closed. Jazz filled the room, shaped shapes from spaces I could not then see, feel. Music filled

the room. Six people, I recognised from the previous party, around the table. Women in backless dresses, they paid little attention to the men, talked amongst themselves. Shrieked with laughter. The men smoked, talked of the navy, army, wars, the war and cars. Dinner over, the table cleared, music turned higher. The women turned towards the men. One of the actors stood over me. You look bored my dear—won't you dance? I left the room and explored the rest of the house.

Each room had the latest fashionable paintings, illuminated from lights under. From the balcony city lights fingered the sky. Cries from street vendors. Voices from outside a restaurant. I walked the length of the balcony. Through glass doors I saw an old man sitting Yoga fashion. Carefully he placed

23

cards in rows. His lips moved behind thin white hairs, a straggly beard. A few whisps caught in his mouth. Over one arm swung a necklace of amber, which he touched, after placing a row of cards. The rows varied in number. He unbent, stroked his beard, the beads. Cards formed a pyramid shape. I moved closer. Many coloured figures spread out in front of him. A half dazed white moth bumped against the window. The old man looked up. I shrank into the shadow, my own, and leaned there. A pool of light splashed on the marble. That part I entered, where I returned. Again behind glass I saw

what did I see, for when that scene reappears it merges with a dream, fallen back into slowly, connected yet not connected in parts. So what I saw then was as much a voyeur's sense. And since has become heightened. Succession of images, controlled by choice. I chose then to remain outside. Later I entered, allowed other entries. In that room a series of pictures thrown on the walls, ceiling, floor, some upsidedown. Only afterwards could I see things. More so now in specific detail. Objects in that room

a wooden fish, mobile, its shadow a crescent moon spinning. Black underwear, boots, whips. A rocking chair rocked. A leather strap strapped round each arm of the chair. A large melon broken open. Red seeds in heaps on the multicoloured floor. A record player near the white marble fireplace. Gutted candles, incense remains, small mountains of thin grey ash. A round broken mirror. Masks on the bed, floor. A white robe, gold braided, draped over the couch, and near the couch a table with cakes. An assortment of jewellery, beads rolled into corners. Strings of beads out of drawers, over the bedpost, chairs. Bracelets amongst fruit, bottles. Wine stains, other stains on costumes. The robes Medieval, Greek, Egyptian, Oriental, surrounded a large circular bed, ornately carved, up one side of the posts a great vine which a centaur clambered. Orchids and other flowers,

24

white, scarlet. Small wooden figures. A crown of vine leaves. Gold and silver sandals. Plants. A large rubber tree plant on its side. Torn scattered petals, leaves. Silk cushions under chairs, between chairs. A tape recorder under a table, microphone near the bed, its cord twisted half under the carpet. A large straw cross lay at the foot of the bed. Blankets in a heap as the three

lay there, their legs, arms linked in the formation of a dance. Under the chandelier they moved slowly. He in the middle hardly moved, watching the two women circle. Their backs arched, breasts thrust high, forward. The leather strap he passed through suspenders. Black slithered across white, between the less black. His head raised, then bent. Arms spread out from the white sleeves. He balanced a whip in each hand. The girl strapped to the chair. Her head swayed over the back, hair hung down. Legs apart, fruit placed between. He drank, but did not swallow. On his knees he thrust his face between. Sound of whip meeting flesh, into a rhythm, slow at first. Merged with the music, as she danced on the table, danced with her shadow, bent back as though to perform a backward somersault, while the other woman behind stretched out both her hands as if to catch the flying figure, and he waited to steady her for when she might land the right way up. She fell away from the fleeting shadows of limbs covered with jewellery. Bracelets round her ankles. His. While she looked in the mirror.

Mirrors faced each other. As the two turned, approached. Slower in movement in the centre, either side of him, turning back in the opposite direction to their first movement. Contours of their shadows indistinct. The first mirror reflected in the second. The second in the first. Images within images. Smaller than the last, one inside the other. She lay on the floor, wrists tied together. She bent back over the chair. He raised the whip, flung into space. In a downward sweep met her legs, back, breasts. Robes long, short, fluttered,

25

were stiff, encircled them. Ends streamed upwards, down, depending on the folds, clinged close about the ankles, separated from them, according as legs were at rest. Material'fitted closely, parted from the limbs. The slow measure within the rhythm he made. Smile spread as he became part of the motion he shaped. She turned towards the shape of his arms. Head over the edge, her hair across. Movement back from the centre to the sides. A hand, two legs in the rising, falling. The light above, below.

The girl's lower lip covered by a fringe of hair. His eyes wide, substances, colours collected. Each thing transmitted the image, receiving all the images of those in front. Scattered light played with fingers, parts of the body. Bodies. Having the same course, in moments contrary, intersecting at right angles, acute angles. His that raised the blanket, fell over the side. The shape of half a ship inverted. Figures on the ceiling, friezes of satyrs, nymphs, centaurs. Nymphs chased by centaurs, satyrs. The girl brought the Egyptian candle-clawed chimera closer. Claws formed candlesticks, held a light, a cupid astride. She danced round, held one claw, balanced there. He hung from the bed. Onto her, from her. Movement above, I moved with, into. The glass pane of yellowish transparency extends now. Cascades of liquid gold, lights, trees, landscape. All seasons passed through before the pattern formed, collected in parts. Dislocated from moment to moment.

Before sleep. After sleep. In dreams. The dream settles into spaces. Divided walls, doors opened out into the sky. The stone I threw into running water, created an oval undulation in two movements. In the clearer water, where shallow, beneath the sun's rays I saw all the shadows, lights of the waves. Things carried by the water. Through the glass, I held, the bowl of flowers, I saw another room, rooms within rooms. Interiors becoming exteriors. A leaf whirled along.

26

Different lines in the water's depth. The surface wave shaped a half circle, at the bottom a quarter circle. Part of the sky closest to the horizon white. White as his hand lifted. That in that room, in the half light then. Behind glass formed a new shape. As ice pinnacles form new shapes. Plants, strange leaves. Shapes the snow forms in the air. Olive trees white. The insects quieter then.

Gusts of wind struck the waters, scooped them out in great hollows, carried up in the shape of a column, the colour of clouds. One great cloud drew to itself smaller ones. Remained stationary, retained the sunlight on its apex, for two hours after the sun had set. Two hours later we sheltered from the storm, above the sea where the water on its bed went in a different direction from that on the surface. We lay in a cave and emerged when the storm seemed calmer. The air still dark from rain that became heavy, fell slantwise, bent by the cross-current winds, formed into waves in the air. The mountain bases covered with debris, shrubs, mud, roots, branches, various kinds of leaves thrust in among the earth, stones. Sand upon the edges of branches. He threw two stones into the pool. I watched the circles increase equally, one within the other, without the one destroying the other. It's getting really cold, he said. So we drove quickly back to the city. From there

we move on.

When, where to decide at what point to preserve

Obsession she has, that at least admitted. Equal to mine?

What are we doing in this city, this land I find no reconciliation with now. Come to terms with that, work it through, out of the system. She says I have no responsibility, no sense of responsibility to myself. I have no quarrel with myself, only an argument to follow through.

Enduring the argument without hope for any answer

Easier letting go when she isn't around. Easier sitting back and thinking. Allow thoughts to go in any direction. Just be in some hotel, part of the room, chairs, table. A little music perhaps. Ah listen to that shaping shapes in space, she said the other afternoon. The light in her eyes, that comes from someone else's eyes. The brightness, lighter movements; the aura she brings back, spreads. I catch some of it, though this sets off the argument. The longing.

Sunday

Heat reflected from the wall across the street. Energetic waiter, almost an Eastern Jew in his gestures. Courtyard noisy as an invasion. Intolerable smells. Mosquito—managed getting three already—crushing this one a hard decision.

Tuesday

Her fantasies: making love on the edge of a bank/ cliff. A space capsule: 'Imagine floating around in all that space and copulating at the same time'. With two men— one under, one above. Another woman.

Almost a relief to be on my own. More and more unable to observe, determine the truth of things, share an experience. Is knowing this as clear as the thing itself? Writing these thoughts, if only to see what I might think. Lucid—well fairly so—at the moment. She has her own lucidity in fantasies, sometimes shared. The need to follow these. The need for sharing mine vicariously.

Note: Does she recognise the sadistic side of my nature?

What have I in common with Jews? I have hardly anything in common with myself.

Monday

The need to find some unambiguous truth—not depending on the edge

No sleep at all, lay two hours in the afternoon sleepless and apathetic. Same at night. Impossible to pull myself together, only when I have become satisfied with the depression can I stop.

On a red-figured Krater: The mad Lycurgus with his children dead and dying. He swings a double axe. A winged mad demon smites the king with her pointed goad. Behind the hill, a Maenad smites her timbrel in token of the presence of the god. On the reverse of vase there's Dionysus, who has made all this madness, looking peaceful. About him are Maenads and Satyrs watching the scene, alert and interested, but in perfect quiet.

Forget everything, open the windows, clear the room. The breeze blows through. I see only the emptiness; I look in all the corners and don't find myself. However within these limits there's space to live, and therefore the possibility to exploit them to a despicable degree.

Jewish couple next door. Her large nose, dark hairline above the mouth, slender body. He shorter, plump, coughs a lot at night. They walk one behind the other in the park opposite the hotel. Their tumbled bed in the morning.

The American couple opposite play cards, watch television all day, half the night. Their neatly made beds in the morning.

Wednesday

Self-pity because it's too hot, because of a hell of a lot of things. Now at seven p.m. someone in the next room kicks off his shoes. Later the bed will creak. And someone hammers a nail in the wall between us.

July

Drowsy fantasies lately.

Forms forming
themselves.
Defining the
centre of things.
No counterpoints.
No intersections/
linears.
Improvisation

View of the temple and blue sky: disrupting.

Sunday

Lay out this obsession: hers/mine:

How she watches
me. God how she
watches herself
watching. How-
ever if no one
observes me I
have to observe
myself all the
more

Obsession/obsidian, obsidional

attention	Carefulness
positiveness	observance
bias	mindfulness
belief	observation
folly	watchfulness
eccentricity	eyes on, watch,
Obsessive/unceasing	guard
habitual	

The general argument: I am completely lost in this country—this climate.

Tuesday

Decision between madness and security is imminent.

Approach of death—madness the only way out?

Depicted on vase: Wheels suspended in Palace of Hades/Persephone. Two kinds solid and spoked.

'I feel as though I'm on loan from the underworld'. Does she expect then for me to play Orpheus? The bleeding head singing always. Divinities of Orphism: demons rather than gods. Development of Orphism doctrine of eternal punishment.

Morbid habit of self-examination. Slayer of Orpheus had a little stag tattooed on upper part of her right arm.

She wore a thin green dress, her legs, thighs showed through. Green against white. She looked flushed. She expected him to ask her something, anything. She sensed his attention elsewhere, the door that opened a crack. The revolver appeared in an outstretched hand.

Later she tried lifting him from the floor, and fell on top. The light spiralled through her hair. Smell of the sea, figs from her hands, made him dizzy, contradicting the terror. The sort that waits at the crack of dawn. An empty bed, when even a cigarette tastes bitter. Waiting for that almighty sun that burns at eight a.m. and the miracle doesn't happen, the miracle he thinks might, yes might occur the next day, when falling into the first part of the euphoria.

Thursday

Ah how much cooler it is
cool
cool

32

cooler. So play it cool. Not wonder if she'll
return before the sun sets. Not measure the
space between where I sit, crouch, bend back
from the table. The space is no distance now.
I can stretch a hand out slowly, be held fascin-
ated by my own fingers.

Not hunger of the
body but of
imagination.
Body an outpost,
boundaries obscure

But soon
soon
soon
sooner than I can anticipate the action she
expects

Darkness already. She hasn't returned. Shirt
soaked, lips dry, eyes bloodshot. 6' 3" of smelly
flesh floating in a foreign city.

> Two cigarettes
> piece of stale cheese
> stale bread
> no ice left

1 a.m.

gull: sense of
fool, may come
from the bird
swallowing any-
thing that's
tossed to it.
Bird name is
common Teut.
Hence also
gullible.

I am vulnerable only as far as another's gul-
libility allows, can contradict this, certainly an
aspect of vulnerability.

2 a.m.

Pursued by memories/visions making the
moment a catalyst. Easy then assuming a likewise role?

33

Almost impossible to sleep; plagued by dreams as if they were carved on me, on a sheet of metal.

She is in her middle thirties, appears younger. Younger without makeup. She looks for her brother, whom she believes came to this country. She is positive she will find him. Meanwhile

She is in her middle thirties, appears younger. at times older. Has the air of a woman who knows her way about. On occasions acts like a child, knows that men are delighted with this image. She's playing at Antigone. This eccentricity she cultivates, wants those she meets to court this.

Saturday

We move with the weather.

Another climate needed. Another place. No sense of place here. Perhaps not even other places. But a place.

How monotonous this blue sky is, she said this morning, without looking out of the window, not looking at anything as she passed over the coffee.

Marking time, playing the games she chooses.

It will change, must change when the rains come.

34

Am I truer to her
than to myself
perhaps?

Seasons/cycles of love

She makes love out of the day's rhythms.

'Don't take me
out of my home',
the girl said,
surrounded by six
starving children
and their excre-
ment.

The political situation here is intolerable.
There's no hope unless a revolution starts.
Bloodshed under clear skies. Such a climate
brings murder/war crimes easily. Restlessness,
can see it all, the way they look, or not look
at us. They still have their rituals their God(s);
their traditions. They have a cause they'll will-
ingly die for. And the women wait, bound up
by their physical approach to things, no illusions, no ideals, wanting to be slaves, knowing
no other role, accepting death as the order of
things.

10th July

Dream

The photograph
on her grave had
a large crack
across it last
time I made a
visit to the
cemetery. I
put a small rock
on top of the
grave.

I am in a cemetery, looking for mother's grave.
The cemetery stretches on all sides to the horizon. I am lying in an open grave, feeling very
content. People, the family (?) throw flowers,
fruit, presents in. Large boxes tied with blue/
purple ribbon. I haul myself up by this. A rope
ladder falls. I am pursued by wild dogs into a
cave. A flock of geese rise, they change into
white horses. I came upon a skeleton, long
white bones. I am struck by their whiteness,
whiter than shells around. I sit there. My father,
dressed as a carnival figure, a kind of crazy
Rabbi, walks along the sea coast. He looks at

35

me, hands me a book, opens his mouth, but says nothing, and walks on. The book falls open on the skeleton. It is the Talmud. I begin to follow my father, the sea rises, cuts me off. Geese/horses cry above me, descend, beat their wings on my head. They start biting, pecking at me. I go back to pick up the Talmud, only the covers remain. The sea sucks at my feet, my genitals. I woke up with an erection.

Different genera and species of dreams

Dreams that structure the day

Dream related
1st and 2nd
consciousness

Dreams interrupted $\left\{ \begin{array}{l} \text{The terrors} \\ \text{of midday} \\ \text{sleep} \end{array} \right.$

Time/space to think back over a dream

Dream accompanied with a sense of touch—single and double touch

Not remembering a dream until something hints at it later in the day/week.

Recapitulating a dream—attempt at interpretation : an exorcise.

Old English :
dream meaning
mirth & minis-
trelsy, died in
14th c. Teut.
draugm—to
deceive.
Old Norse :
draugr, ghost.

The horror that lingers, sensing some prediction/premonition : a crisis/death/loss.

An unsatisfactory embodiment of what I intended.

Drawing of third
Siren's eye by
two strokes only,
without the pupil:
the sightless eye,
eye in death/
sleep/blindness.

Image of myself
as Bar-Lgura, the
Semetic demon
sitting on the
roof and leaping
down on them all.

My last words to
her: 'there are
maggots in the
mincepie'.

As it is the
custom to do:
telling his
mother's name,
which is part of
his 'true' name,
is an essential
part of the
procedure in which
a hasid opens his
heart to a zaddik.

Sometimes she talks in her sleep. Names I don't know. Some secret language. She says I talk Hebrew in my sleep, yet I only know a few words in that language. There are moments when she looks at me startled, not really seeing me, perhaps thinking I am someone else. The walls shift in patterns, colour, shapes behind her head, and I think I am somewhere else. At home perhaps, when the murmurs are Mother's, made from her bed, the light shining from the kitchen, stopping in a blade of light at the foot of the bed. How I hated Mother then. Day after day (and nights, long nights) of pain. Windows closed, curtains pulled, thin-walled box rooms. Death, the smell of it, of sickness permeated everything. Nurses, doctors came and went, she thought were the family. I made her hot drinks, and thought of pissing in them. I wanted to screw my sister in front of her and Father. I hated her then for allowing death to cheat her as likewise life. The sunken eyes looked up with incomprehension from the damp sheets. I was convinced then that change could introduce no sense of renewal; I feared death, seeing it for the first time. Father I still see, sitting there, opening the Book of Esther, flicking off a squashed bug, reading in a monotonous tone, possibly thinking of his mistress waiting. Waiting, then no longer: within a year they married. For a week I thought of rising at sunrise, thought of the custom I could not betray myself to: reading the Kaddish in mourning for a whole year.

She envies my Jewish blood, no reason, at least

37

she said there wasn't any specific one. Envy for the historical sense of it all, a meaning for feeling persecuted? Strangely enough I've felt more Jewish with her curiosity than I've ever felt before. Though usually I feel no more Jewish than

lover
husband
brother
father
guardian
prophet
mystic
writer
addict
= demi-god
= beast

Can be any one of these, according to whim/projection. What is it/ shall it be for today

'The scape-goat stood all skin and bone
While moral business, not his own,
Was bound about his head'.

Hebrew Conception:
The scape-goat was not a sacrifice proper: its sending away was preceded by sacrifice.

'And the goat shall bear upon him all their iniquities into a land not inhabited'.

On the train

Something about getting completely high while mobile, not subjected to one's own mobility. Fantastic dance of images, shapes, forms. Shadows flowing past. She stands in the doorway, her face thinner, slightly flushed (how it can change!). She looks as if expecting something to happen, for me to say something. Her

38

eyes wander from mine to the window, and back again. Rumble of wheels, a sudden stirring of birds rising out of trees. Her laughter that doesn't come, though her mouth is open. Maybe she's about to cry. Maybe

What of madness —can one take on another's. What would it be like to get completely outside our bodies?

'We are mediums inhabiting each others' imagination'.

My own madness: not swift enough, slow moving to/ away from the edge. She likes to think people look upon her as essentially quite mad, almost a prerequisite for any lover she has.

Swift hounds of raging madness : Bacchae

She   What are you thinking?
He   Why you are still with me
She   Because I'm mad

He smiles. Silence. They look out of the window. He watches the dust stirred by a passing vehicle. The sun in the dust, dust in the sun. Women pass, water jugs on their heads, they pause, one hand balanced lightly on the jugs, they watch the train. She watches him. Waits.

Madness of Dionysus includes the madness of the Muses and Aphrodite.

A sculptured slab : Design of the Birth of Aphrodite. Two women support her, and to whom in her

She   Did you say something?
He   No
She   Oh I thought you did

uprising she clings. They stand on a sloping bank of shingle. Between the edges of the bank there's no indication of the sea, simply a straight line.

He coughs. Her hand passes lightly, swiftly through her hair, bracelet, rings, runs her finger along a ladder starting, ending at the knee

He   Like a drink?
She Not particularly
He   Mind if I do?
She Go ahead

He lifted the bottle to his dry lips, and saw himself quite clearly in that moment as she must see him often: heavy, blotched, air of uncertainty in hotel corridors, trains, streets, harbours, waiting rooms, parks. Suspicious, hostile. Persistent talking in idiot fashion, or worse: insistent silence, preoccupied with concerns she would call indulgent, metaphysical, calculating. He straightened up, straightened his tie, and hoped he gave her his 'High Priest' look. 'If there's such a thing as reincarnation I see you as a kind of Priest somewhere in the time B.C.'. He enjoyed the look of passiveness, of sacrifice that came into her eyes. But soon he realised this was hardly 'submission' to the image, but one of curiosity to see if he had anticipated the next image she had in store for him.

A Hellenistic relief: Right-hand corner is a herm, in front of this an altar, nearby a tree on which hangs a votive syrinx. A traveller has fallen asleep. Down upon him has pounced a winged bird-footed woman.

Diary of The Separated Woman

Condition without future?

'I love all men, how can I ever be tied to one man for the rest of my life?'.

She lives with/from her passions
She wants to recapture her youth, not accepting she has lost hers. She makes love with men
younger than herself (the age her brother
disappeared?).

Medusa in her
essence is a head,
nothing more:
her potency only
begins when her
head is severed,
and that potency
resides in the
head; a mask with
a body later
appended.

Her beauty lies in her emotions, fleeting, changing in her face, eyes. Mobile. The promise
of . . .

Sunday

A short dream while dozing, clung to it with
delight. A dream of many offshoots, full of a
dozen connections becoming clear in a moment;
but hardly more than the mood/tone remains.

Tuesday

Sirens, mantic
creatures, like
the Sphinx,
knowing past and
future. Their
song takes effect
at midday, in a
windless calm.
They dwell on an
island in a
flowery meadow.

Girls, boys rise, their bodies dark rich brown.
They go down, come up from the beach, laughing, for no apparent reason than liking the
sound of their own laughter. Laughter turning
into song. God knows I envy their lightness.
Their despair: a certain kind of despair only
the young have: irrational, inconsistent.

41

Depression
lowness
depth
valley
descent
psychopathy
adversity
poverty
nervousness

Refusing to whom
—oneself
    ?
Refusing the
possibilities
the chance
that . . .

The indulgence
    evasion
    excuses
Attitude of cynicism
Quiet intolerance
Making love coldly/
    clinically
Refusing to go out
Insomnia

Self-pity
arrogance
resignation
wanting
demanding
reassurance
Wearing old clothes
Not washing/shaving
    for days
Going into some
    unknown bar

Seeing everything through, extending possibilities/limitations, until these seem exhausted, and all that's left is a backward movement: delayed reaction.

Service of the underworld is not all aversion, there's also some element of tendance.

She says she knows no limits in/for herself.

How much a dynasty of approbation does any man need, how far does his 'wanting' command forces towards sexual indulgences.
And woman's vanity: the need to be wanted?

Jealousy: the need now for unmotivated jealousy. However . . .

Jealousy gave to the Satyrs their horns, manes, tusks and tails.

Aggressive love of the mother
Competitive love of the father
The struggle with these images, the destruction, finally an anguished compromise (on both sides?).

42

'Anxiety makes me generous'.

I try to kill my passions. To find a kind of balance would be more natural.

August

A longing for other cities. Cities I haven't been in before. Some hotel where each room is different. A cooler more temperate climate. The weather weathers my outlook. Making love with someone, quiet contained passion, knowing we'll never make love again, nor see each other. Disastrously spoilt when the woman 'phones up the next day, and the next; perhaps starts accusing, crying. I give in, we meet, we make love, it's not the same. She knows this, but continues believing it is as it was, that the 'affair' can be perpetuated. Then the letters arrive. At first short, sweet, finally 'you son of a bitch' tone. Then the guilt that brings anger.

A black-figured lekythos:
Colossal head and lifted hands of a woman rise from the earth. Two men either side of her, armed with hammers, one of the men strikes the woman's head.

'The problem is I never want to begin an affair, at least not get that involved, equally nor do I want to end, when at times quite by accident I am involved'. She said the other night, making her usual faces in the mirror.

The illusion she creates is the most real thing for her. The dress she wears becomes the foundation of the part she'll play, and he'll take his cue from there.

Her faces:

Mature woman
  Subtle in talk and/or silences
  Languid in movements
  Not chain-smoking (though might smoke a small cigar).

43

Order only expensive exotic drinks—likewise food.

Femme Fatale
 Teasing
 Flirtatious
 Quick
 Witty
 Mysterious smiles
 Wears false lashes and hair piece
 Appears to know all the secrets/perversions of love/love making, and will by the way she gestures, smiles, promise all, then laughing suddenly withdraw and dance with someone else.

Often she gets pretty high then she forgets which role she had started with, and a delightful mixture of them all appears, leaving the man confused or even more infatuated.

The Mystic
 Soulful
 Wistful
 Pensive
 Given to sudden moods of inward concentration
 Long deep gazes
 Deep sighs
 Half smiles
 Talks of ESP/projections
 Relates strange experiences.

Country girl 'at heart'
 Walks without shoes, usually by the sea
 Swims naked
 Lets the wind toss un-sprayed hair
 No makeup
 Admires a strange or familiar bird—making the strange familiar and vice versa.
 Picks wild flowers

Sees strange designs/faces in stones, rocks
and trees
Hardly talks, but will suddenly say things
like 'have you ever made love in the snow
without clothes—imagine in a snowdrift, to
come in all that whiteness and the glow
afterwards!'.

Mentioned I had
once, but with
clothes on. She
gave an amused
look, then lost
interest.

From a black-
figured cylix:
a large dog, of
supernatural size,
almost the height
of a man. To the
left of him a
bearded man is
hastening away,
apparently in
surprise or
consternation.
Immediately
behind the dog
comes a winged
figure, also in
haste, and mani-
festly interested in
the dog. Behind
her is Hermes, and
behind him, as
quiet spectators
two women.

They couldn't bear it a moment longer. They
knew that they were being followed. Despite it
being the middle of the night they ran away.
Mountains encircled the city. They climbed up
them and set all the trees shaking as they swung
down from one to the other.

Monday

White heat. Whiteness of buildings. The dark
line of trees. Such open sky between mountains, over the sea.

Wednesday

To be on the move again at least is something.
She feels we are being watched: 'Perhaps they
think we are spies'.

45

In his anger he
strangled the
dog who slept
in his lap

The Arabs sacri-
ficed to the
morning star boys
of special beauty
and slew them at
dawn on a heap of
piled-up stones.
When supply of
boys ran out they
took a white
camel, bent it
down on its knees,
circled round it
three times. After
third circuit the
priest smites the
camel's neck
and eagerly tastes
the blood. Finally
no scrap of the
victim is uneaten
that might be seen
by the rising sun.

Look of intense hatred on the interpreter's face
when I gave him the money finally. The
pleasure I felt! Unlike the complexities´ of
guilt/anger gone through when confronted by
beggars, whether I give them anything or not.

In the upstairs room the guard made advances
A young boy. I led him to
believe he was
beautiful
superior
that I was drunk
that the woman being questioned was a whore
I had picked up the night before
that in short I was a kind of tragic dilettante.

Friday

Glorious light over this harbour. Landscape
bathed in luminous colour, spreads through the
room. Pins me to the bed.

Mysterious disappearance of a man wearing a
seersucker suit and straw hat, and his mysterious reappearance on the train.

Sunday

She returned at sunrise, offered me some melon.
The mark on her neck, where the hair parted

46

near the mole, curiously resembled the melon
I sucked. Later I bought her some flowers, the
same colour, the plastic/wax kind they put on
graves on the small crosses on mountainsides.

Ten spiral staircases round a tower
The temple :
        twelve flights of steps
        800 ft in circumference
        Built in the shape of an octagon
        Eight large pillars rising 24ft above base
           of plinth
        Above each angle a large pillar
        Between the pillars interposed are ten
           columns (same height as the pillars)
           rising 28½ft above pavement
        Toward the centre rise pillars and
           columns corresponding to the eight
           pillars of the angles, and the columns
           placed in the facade.

On a vase:
Series of men with
fish tails. A
Horse-Satyr pipes
on the double
flutes. Worshipper
of Dionysus.

No leave me alone no no let me be. He
shouted all the way through the streets, and
again she laid hold of him, again and again
the clawed hands of the siren struck at his
head from the side or across his neck.

Mid-August

Strange party last night when I lost sight of
her half way through. There were so many
rooms. I went in search through the ornately
furnished house (bad imitation stuff: tapestries

47

/paintings/vases—a few genuine perhaps).
Later I saw her dress fluttering behind a bench,
a man's leg round her, at least I thought it was
her. I could have been mistaken. Her dress was
torn, she had seaweed, sand in her hair when
we left.

Sunday

The endless shining of the sun. Meanwhile the
cocks crow day and night. Their persistent
crowing. And my own.

'You want to be
a saint I think
that's your
problem. Ah
what arrogance
in hoping you'll
ever reach a
state of grace'.

She had no other description than that the man
was a black-beretted lieutenant. I think she is
seeing him tonight. I no longer question, at least
not question her motives. And mine?

The man was writing in the middle of the
garden; blotched face, unshaven, long hair
brushed straight back. Rigid stare, looked right
and left out of the corners of his eyes. The
paper he had been writing on blew off. The
paper had a drawing of a centaur about to carry
off a winged siren.

Tuesday

There are possibilities certainly, but from what
stone do they crawl under?

Terror in the merely schematic.

48

Portrait of a Man in Search of Perfection

'I only wish to dominate desire'.

'I try to be objective because basically I distrust freedom'.

'Perhaps the Minotaur is after all charming, like Caliban, I feel sorry for him—no —compassion yes is better, for what can it be like to be born of unmention- able monstrous- ness, never to know the delights of love/ loving?'. She said on their last night together, the sheets damp with sweat, tears, their lovemaking.

Depicted on a seal impression:
A Minotaur with horned bull-head, pronounced bovine ears and tail.
He is seated on a throne, of camp- stool shape, before him is a worship- per. His left leg crossed human fashion over right knee, human hands extended.

Their affair came to an end when the wife finally left. How much did they lean on her, she on them? She perhaps gave them the limi- tation to their love, and when she was no longer there . . .

Who could consent to their indulgences? But it was the women who made their decisions, who left him. He had been, after all, quite happy having them both, could see no reason why the one rather than the other. This they called 'evasion'. So they acted, being 'strong' superior women. He, for a time, enjoyed the aspect of being 'the man whose wife and mistress had given up'—ah reminds me of my bachelor days. There seemed countless choices before him. He travels, teaches. He makes love, non-committed on both sides. He writes a book, that turns out a great success. He travels, lectures, and goes to academic parties, flirts entertainingly with Professorial wives/daugh- ters. He marries again. He could be called 'the successful man'; yet still he faces the mirror and says: Where did it all go wrong?

Saturday

Don't get bogged down, risk all, what is there but the risking? So. She risks with her body, her imagination (her heart/mind?).

49

Ah the light the light how beautiful it is—look do look. She flung up the blinds, and pulled the covers from my face this morning. Two mornings ago? Three/four perhaps five days/nights lying, sitting here in this unbearable heat. Where the compulsion, the impulse, the desire to go out, for say a swim? She returns each morning just after the sun has risen, bathed in smoothness from the sea, from someone's caresses. She fondles herself. She tidies the room, the bed, not with disgust. Nothing. Not even pity. (I've put the sign Please Do Not Disturb outside the door—the thought of the maid bustling in with brooms, duster etc., sends me into a fantastic terror). Her thoughts elsewhere as she bends, hums, and places the coffee near the bed, but not near enough this morning, so that it was an effort, ah this effort to reach out, consequently I knocked the cup over. Then she shouted: Jesus why don't you get up and have at least a shower you smell of Godknowswhat.

Ah how you hug happiness with jealousy—the price to pay— (what puritanism!).

Facing the sun would be something. So I got up, washed, shaved, dressed. At last presentable, upright for the upsidedown world. I went into the nearest bar. The time went, things assumed confirmation. I felt benevolent, listened to some prostitute's life story, and actually, yes really so, felt sorry for her, and bought her drinks, yet I knew what she said was a complete fabrication, but she believed it at the time, as much as I did, in the half light then.

That something will happen— a world of happenings, of shapes assuming transparent luminous quality. Thin as air, as light as spray.

I went back to her place, gave her some more

money. I might have had her, except there were two children there. I rather fancied the daughter, her mother soon realised this, and pushed the child, who couldn't have been more than twelve, towards me; unbuttoned the girl's blouse, fondled the small breasts. I derived as much pleasure from watching her do this as if I had actually felt their firmness, the brown nuts I wanted to crack open.

A boy in rags, an idiot I thought at first, played with a piece of string, sang, laughed the whole time. I got up to leave, then noticed the boy had no legs. Meanwhile the woman had completely undressed the girl, who stood painfully in the middle of the cluttered smelly room, small fingers in greasy hair. She was really too thin. The boy played a flute, the girl bent back, legs wide apart, danced round me. Fuzz of her pubic hairs held my attention for a while. The woman begged for some more money. I refused. She spat on the floor. The girl crouched next to her brother, who continued playing squeaky loud notes. The woman screamed. I left and stumbled over cripples in passage ways, alleys. The thought of knives thrown at my back made me continually turn round, but the beggars only held out their withered hands, plates. I wanted then to leave the city, find more open space. I walked by the sea, even in the dunes, there seemed grotesque shapes appearing, crawling towards me.

I saw myself suddenly in a mirror, and the white body of the girl. That whiteness blinding me. The whiteness whiter than I could ever remember white to be.

Retinal fantasies: Knives—dazzling knives spinning through space. Motionless caught in moonlight. A madman's eye plucked out—a centipede stuck to a rock, pinned there by a burning knife.

Carcasses. Corpses of another civilisation.

The immense endless sea of eyes. Bodies. Insects without heads.

Dream

A glass stairway I climb into the sky, changes
into a bank of snow. I collapse. My body
covered by fish scales, fins, tails, I try picking
off. I swim in snow. I am a star fish. I dance
underwater, between arrows of light that pierce
the ripples, waves above. Through me. I float
between stars, between the sun and moon. A
centipede settles on the sun, I squash it with
a starfish feeler. It blackens the sun with dark
blood that drips onto my head, eyes. Hot blood
like oil. It is oil. I plunge into water. It is ice.
I sink into the ice. A woman bends over me.
My head sticks out of the ice. I lick the woman,
the pinkness, wet, dripping. My mouth full of
fish. I go down into transparency. I am alone.
I cry out in halls of icicles. I crawl towards an
opening, a shaft of light that gradually dark-
ens. The sun and moon have been blotted out
by a thousand and one centipedes.

She wondered why for the first time in ages I
jumped out of bed this morning, and pushed
open the shutters, stood for a long time in the
sunlight. Even though I had to shut my eyes, it
was a relief to feel that hot sun on my body,
my face. See the spots, sparks of light behind
eyelids. But the dream pursues me, like some
odour. Almost the desire to go back over, back
into it, perhaps extend, likewise the dream I
had last month.

The day deceives me—already it is night.

Cut-up dream

I am walking in a glass stairway. I climb into
the sky, mother's grave. The cemetery a bank of
snow. I collapse. All sides to the horizon. Body
covered by fish scales in the open grave. I swim
in snow. The family throw flowers, star-fish. I
dance underwater, between arrows in large
boxes, tied with light that pierce the ripples,
waves above. I haul myself up. I float between
stars, between ladders. I am pursued by the sun
and moon. A centipede settles on the cave. A
flock of geese blacken the sun with blood that
drips. White horses come onto my head, eyes. I
plunge into hot blood, oil, white bones. Ice
whiter than shells. A woman bends over me.
My father dressed as a carnival. The pinkness,
wet, dripping. My mouth full of crazy Rabbi,
walks along the fish. I go down into transparency. Father looks at me, hands me a book.
Alone I cry out in halls of icicles. I say nothing, and walk on. I crawl towards a shaft that
opens onto a skeleton. I begin to follow my
father. Geese/horses cry above. The sun and
moon beat their wings on my head. They have
been blotted out by a thousand and one centipedes, feet, my genitals.

Fold-in time/order/space

Function of the whole score is to establish the
language.

53

Light on the horizon: nostalgia

Midday light: loneliness

Trail of plane broken off in wide expanse of
blueness: memories

Trail of seaweed after the tide has turned:
panic.

Earth-born
goddesses, though
they shed their
snake form, keep
as their vehicle
and attribute the
snake they once
were.

Poverty of these people; they live often in nothing but hovels, however they have fantastic
pride, and on the whole very cheerful. Most of
the land well cultivated. The harvest festival
held in a small village, we went to this afternoon, full of dancing, singing men and women.
The great round threshing floor filled with
swaying bodies. They had worked hard at the
cutting of corn, the threshing, afterwards win-
nowed in the open threshing-floor. A booth had
been erected nearby where the performers
rested, ate and drank in the intervals of their
pantomimic dancing. An old man stood behind us, a newborn baby in his arms. 'We must
have him quickly baptized for if we don't he
may at any moment disappear in the form of
a snake'. He gestured with his gnarled fingers,
making quick weaving movements between us,
followed by the sign of the cross. Ah they are
still so superstitious. She said afterwards, frown-
ing. Later I wanted to ask her what had happened with the priest she had seen, if she had

found out anything useful. She seemed so pre-occupied. Finally she said there was a certain island we must go to, a cemetery she wanted to see.

Saturday

The island proved to be less cultivated than most, than those we passed in the boat. It was still volcanic, and had suffered an eruption a few years ago. Ruins everywhere. The cemetery was not kept up, difficult therefore to read the names. She thought we might even then be walking on top of her brother. We went on over dry earth, stones, rocks, weeds. Carrions flew up onto branches, watched us in silence the whole time. We stayed longer on the island than intended, mainly because of the hospitality of a war veteran and his sister. I must admit the girl didn't attract me in the least, with her dyed red hair, swarthy skin, though she did have a very beautiful body, once naked, which made up for the rest, the stumpy legs covered with black hairs. I gave her some money after-wards, which she refused. She pleaded for us to take her away from the island, from her brother, who I think made use of her, there not being any available women in the village. He seemed jealous, but at the same time collabor-ated with me, saying 'she pleases you—she wants you—she would make you a good woman'. This said when we were by ourselves walking through vineyards. Found myself con-tinually surprised at the dexterity of his stumps, lighting a match, eating, the gestures he made

Among the Libyan tribe of the Nasamones, tombs were used for the taking of oaths and dream oracles —by touching the tombs, and they divine there, regularly resort-ing to the monuments of their ancestors, and having made supplication they go to sleep. Whatever vision they behold of that they make use.

55

with them (he had picked up a hand grenade—arms immediately blown off). She said she felt sorry for him, but felt frightened not so much of his deformity, but of his insistence. We had to eventually steal out of the house. We found a fisherman to take us back to the mainland. Endless endless journey in that midday heat.

Random love: the realisation now that there's no longer the same excitement. Sex alone: dull, and yet—yet the pleasure of making love with the strange gypsy woman from the cafe, completely abandoned, like some wild dance, the feeling of devouring, being devoured. Smell of her body, hair linger. The variety in her amazed and frightened me. I felt vulnerable, yet superior at the same time.

Bird-woman = a death demon, a soul sent to fetch a soul, a Ker that lures a soul.

From a Kotylos: funeral mound decorated with a huge snake with dropped jaw and beard. Two men seated, watch the portent of the eagle and the snake.
Reverse of vase to the right of the tomb mound decorated with a stag, and the portent is an eagle devouring a hare.

Grave number 2,567 in the cemetery of one of the city's suburbs.

The tensions were building up between them, as much as the wind that continued rising. She wanted to scream and/or for him to make some gesture of warmth. He, confused by her earlier outburst, the continuing weight of her mood, remained stiff and aloof. She looked at him, darting bird-like glances, and knew he was about to say something. She waited almost breathlessly for his words, and then: Will be heavy rain tonight. She collapsed back again into the weight, he into his, perched there, staring at the half finished meal.

Mid-week
4 a.m.

Just returned from a wild party—crazy in the sense that I felt so high, and still do, without having had all that much to drink. That she went on ahead, admittedly was my idea, and still she doesn't know I went to the party later. I was aware of her, in fact felt sure I saw her on several occasions in other rooms, and out on the balcony. I thought I heard someone, saw a face flattened against the window, when looking past the two women lying either side of me.

Now writing this, I even wonder that in fact she didn't come into the room, perhaps joined us. There was so much movement there in that room. The singing, dancing, rhythm of the whip I held, and the movements of that, the sound striking.

I had decided to make the party completely on my own, but then the idea of taking the woman from the cafe struck me as something that might prove exciting. She said she would go if

57

her father joined us. He was an old man, who spoke very little, at first I thought him dumb. He eventually spoke, but in a dialect I didn't understand. I was a little worried what the others at the party might make of this strange trio turning up, fortunately everyone was too drunk to even witness our arrival, notice what went on.

The old man had a pack of Tarot cards, his daughter said he could tell my fortune, she would interpret. I suggested some other time, some other place. We left him sitting on the floor, on a Persian carpet, dealing the cards out for God knows who. The woman, even now I don't know her name—it does not matter—disappeared. I wondered if she would come back. I went through many rooms, past many people, some sitting quietly, others lying on the floor, the lawns, eating, drinking, laughing, dancing, making love. The woman appeared with a young girl.

We climbed the spiral staircase to the top of the house, and found a large vacant room. The woman opened a pill box, with many compartments, some filled with aromatic herbs, and round, oblong coloured pills. She handed me one. I asked her what it was, what it might do. She smiled, nodded, her arms like large wings came out at me, over me. I took the pill.

The women lay on the bed and caressed each other. I felt amused, and gradually more and more excited. They danced round me. The girl naked under a transparent dress, and the

The Bacchai
hold orgies in
honour of a mad
Dionysus, they
celebrate a
divine madness
by the eating
of raw flesh.
The final
accomplishment
of their rite is
the distribution
of the flesh of
butchered
victims, they
are crowned with
snakes and
shriek out the
name 'Eva'.

The sacra of
the Dionysiac
mysteries:
a ball, a mirror,
a cone.

I seemed to be on
the interior
within forms and
shadows—wonder-
ing when they
become real: not
knowing who's the
medium for whom.
medium for their
mediums.
Whether I was the

woman, her breasts bared, cut open a melon, held grapes, sucked them, and rubbed herself on me, under me. She bound the girl to a rocking chair, and handed me the whip. At first I felt foolish, not quite knowing what to do, what was expected. The pill must have started working at that point. I handled the whip, her body as though they were the most natural things in the world, something I had always done. Perhaps in retrospect the most exciting part of all this was not so much my whipping the girl, but seeing her so abandoned, submissive and obviously getting more and more excited, roused under me, under the strokes I dealt. At the beginning these strokes were gentle. I saw myself in a mirror the woman held next to us. Soon she put the mirror down, and knelt, took me in her mouth, while I continued whipping the girl, my fingers inside her, while she rocked backwards, forwards, her head over the chair, long hair swung down, later swung over me, over my feet she sucked.

She put bracelets round my arms, ankles, and danced to some Indian music that came up from the gardens. I opened the doors leading to the balcony, and it was then I thought I saw someone run along. I called out, but the women pulled me back in, onto the bed. One lay on top of me, the other on top of her. They seemed more intent on the rituals, the preliminaries of this scene than actually wanting me to enter them. I enjoyed this, enjoyed the anticipation until it no longer seemed to matter whether I entered or not, one or the other, or both. Their madness I entertained, and by this madness equally entertained; it seemed something I had known in some other time, some other life. The room, furniture, the objects familiar. The friezes around, when it seemed the figures depicted on these came to life and joined us.

I fell asleep, and woke up hanging over the bed. The room, the house silent, empty. The women had gone, there was not a trace they had ever been there, except for the strong smell of herbs, incense. I wondered then if I had dreamed the whole scene, until I saw the whip swinging over the rocking chair, that still rocked, only gently then as I sat up, dazed, and saw the other things. The plates of half-eaten fruit, fruit squashed on the floor. And the straw cross they had used in their caresses with each other, with myself. The cross was the only thing I took with me, it lies now on the desk before me.

I can hear the insects of the night, wind through cypresses, and the sea not very far away. Now her steps along the corridor. She enters. What will she say—it does not matter, no longer matters. God I'm exhausted. That is all she says as she goes to her bed. Soon we will pack our cases, leave once again, and move on. Move to another place. Another city where perhaps . . .

A PLACE NOW. The bay where islands appear, vanish, reappear. Plane trees, mountains. Counterpoints, contradictions, improvisation in roles we assume. Shape

of his body. Hair parted half way from the crown. A dark line spreading from the belly. Spine. At such times I nearly forget, call him by another name. There seems little choice, when the possibilities of finding my brother prove negative. He is no longer startled. We walked up a bank. Along the cliff I stumbled. I called out. He walked on, his head bent against the wind. She grazed the upper part of her right arm. He held her by the elbow as they walked slowly back to the hotel.

Another hotel I can't get attached to, he said, stuffing newspaper into the keyhole. I wiped the blood from my arm. Lips. He bent over writing on the balcony, now and then looking up. An old woman tossed crumbs to gulls. I heard their wings. His hands waved in the space between as he talked. This climate is quite unbearable—how long must we endure it? He leaned back, rocked himself, arms folded. He squinted at the sea. Look at those kids down there they are starving yet still they play their games. He took a photograph. She stood against the white railings. It will be a good one I think—got the gulls and that woman—the children in the background. The photo white, face expanded, hand a small rock against blur of railings, sky. Gull wings on the woman's head in a white land uninhabited. The sea simply a straight line.

The other photograph I no longer take out. Description adequate enough. But in that describing, at times, I lose track, as in relating a dream. The sense of touch, single, double touch in the identity conjured after midday sleep. Half awake, two strokes from a distant clock. My eyes sightless, until focusing on some object near. My own hand. His eyes in sleep. Mauve veins of the eyelids. My face a mask, body later attached.

I walked onto the roof. He listened to the children singing. Watched a paralysed girl brought up a sloping bank of shingle, two women supported her. He fell asleep under a tree, woke up slowly and related a dream. He had raped the girl. He said something about this being a condition without future. What is without future? He questioned me, laughing. No sense of sharing this. His dream. He often sees himself as the scape-goat. This according to some whim in moments. Including the madness he almost wants. Her madness he no longer questioned. Made her feel less mad. More mad. Exaggeration of moods played out. His face white, twitched. Tears from eye corners met the corners of his mouth. I'm not crying you needn't think that—just yawning, he said, stretched out under the almond trees

on an island. A flowery meadow where I picked flowers, all those surrounding us and the trees. Grass. Sound of grass against feet. I scattered the flowers about his head. I was not swift enough. He threw them over the clearing, where they dropped on the skin, bones of some bird. An eagle. Can you hear the sirens—listen, he said, his head to one side. Listen can you hear them—their song is supposed to take effect at midday. The wind, south by south wind through the branches. Waves broke in a lowness.

The descent we took led us past a gypsy camp. A woman and child approached with lifted hands. The child's feet and hands bruised, bleeding. I gave them money. They followed us, begged for more. He threw some coins. The child ran some distance, picked up the scattered money, he was swift then returning. More children, shouting, ran towards us. He shook his head, and walked quickly on. She was surrounded. Girls, babies at their breasts, looked on from an outer circle, stared at her clothes, jewellery. She pushed the children away and ran, shouting out for him. The woman I had given the money to started screaming. Two men either side of her, one hit her on the side of the head. The other wrenched her hands open and took the money. They ran off through the trees.

He leaned against a wall, his eyes half closed. Expression on his face, around his mouth, not his own it seemed. Or was it the light, shadows falling across his face. They live with their emotions and on those of others—they think we are fools giving them that much money—see look what happens. He said, pulling up a blade of grass, he chewed. Squinted up at her. He took the grass, stringy out of his mouth. Well you have your illusions and I'm not going to take those away for what would be left. She smoothed her hair, clothes, touched her necklace, bracelet, rings, and watched the flight of many birds move into various designs over the sea. Specks against the horizon. Confused there, perhaps by a stronger wind, they spread out. Specks

on blotting paper trailed across. Doodles he made, while on the telephone. She made from these chance shapes, patterns, things that might assume predictable forms. They were

63

thin as air, light as the spray she felt against her face, legs. They walked from the harbour, and sat outside a bar. He attentive to his drink, newspaper. Slender legal rights for people held as political suspects—ah the situation is definitely deteriorating—who's to know your brother might have been one of these—missing possibly shot dead while trying to escape—are you feeling all right would you like to go back —or another drink perhaps—something to eat?

His left leg crossed over right knee, hands extended either side of the paper. And the other, with blonde thin hairs on his wrists, slightly damp. She walked near enough so that her dress touched the back of his chair. She heard the rustle of newspaper, felt his eyes on the nape of her neck. The blow there. The coolness of his gaze. I try to be objective about these things you know nevertheless the situation could prove quite dangerous—I mean for us—the power of the security police is growing—we may have to get out of the country fairly soon before they have the chance of deporting us to that island—many are apparently held there indefinitely. She nodded, her attention caught by the other's fingers around the glass stem. A light caught the light on the glass, in there, on the stone, in a ring. Newspaper folded on the table. He pecked at pieces of meat, looked at each piece as if for something else. She knew he was a foreigner.

He acknowledged her in the hotel by smiling a half smile. He did not seem to belong, belong in his clothes. Were they too large, too small? Something was wrong somewhere. Perhaps the tie with that shirt. She sat in the lounge. He at the bar. She saw him in the mirror. She looked at a magazine. Cigarettes lit one from another. His fingers round the stem of glass again. I felt sure something would happen. I ordered a drink. He lit my cigarette. Don't you think this place is after all charming? He said, fingers sliding across the lighter, again and again. She found herself breathless, could not,
64

would not answer. But she smiled, less than half a smile. He was after all a stranger, a foreigner. Someone she would prefer not to know. Besides . . .

They went for a swim. The water warmer than expected. He lay a few yards away. His clothes neatly folded between them. Trousers, jacket obviously bought in the city. He had perhaps never worn anything similar before. They had not taken the shape of his limbs. Limbs that fitted comfortably into uniform. His arms behind his head. He wore large sunglasses. She knew he watched her movements. Movements she might make. Not make. By accident his foot rested against hers. She lay motionless, and waited. She saw

him against a heap of piled up stones, bent down on his knees. A white camel about to struggle up. She circled him three times. After the third circuit she laughed. Her hair fell across his eyes. Over one side of her face. He pointed at the morning star. Someone played the double flutes in the distance. A horse neighed, sounds of dogs, that had barked the night through, joined the angry voices, noises of those waking up.

A starfish floated in on the tide. He touched with a branch. It remained still. Something else he poked at, stuck to a rock, pinned there. He eventually removed. The stain of this on the rock, sand. His foot covered. We ran into a cave, listened to the rain fall on rocks, the sea. Waves on the shore. Gull cries on some storm-tossed fish. Later the eagle devoured a hare.

Faces, bodies, insects caught, spun in space, the night I returned. Alone. He had to meet his fiancee at the airport. He was very much in love. Or so he said, and good luck— and well thank you. He gave me a photograph. He had since grown a beard. I was not sure it was a photo of him at all.

I put the photo with the rest when I reached the hotel.

He lay on the floor. I thought he was in some kind of stupor. One eye opened slowly, a madman's eye. He spoke of a death demon, said he had celebrated a divine madness. His body had not belonged to him, did not know how to occupy it again. Of feeling a victim of my medium at times. I watched him closely. At a distance. His eyes wide. I think that's your problem you know hoping to reach a state of divine madness, he shouted, sat up, clutched his knees. I saw him behind glass, his hands round the woman. The whip raised. The sharing of this, though we never spoke of it. I guess I only wish to dominate, he continued, do you think I'm mad—have I killed someone—is there someone dead—I feel I am your brother.

From the balcony I saw the whiteness of waves lift over, spread along the coast. The mountains, their darkness where clouds must have rested. His hands came out, their whiteness flashed in the mirror. I began dancing through rooms. I saw the girl's body he had raped, she was no longer paralysed, but danced, then knelt in front of him. You see I am a High Priest after all, he said, bent over me. My hair across his feet. I don't know whether I'm going more into your mind or you into mine, he whispered. I sank back. He clutched my thighs, twitched, grasped. I wanted to laugh. What happens when something psychic becomes an exaggeration? He looked up, spoke slowly then. I have entered a new world I can accept the conditions the built in illusions—can you hear me? I half closed my eyes and saw someone at the window, space behind illuminated. A gold bar across the window. A person, shadow behind this. Two flowers, Lotus opened. A white tree stripped of leaves, floated. Am I speaking in cliches? He asked, then relapsed into silence, eyes closed, his body limp.

I lay on the bed. The beach. On a rock, pinned under him.

In the cave. Sound of water passing through other caves. Under the mountains. Distant sound of thunder and the barking of dogs. Nothing I've written matters I just want to live —are you listening? He sat on the edge of the bed, and stared at the wall, beyond the wall, many walls. Rooms, landscapes I entered, travelled there before him. Always he was there. The blonde hairs, the slender

shadows of almond trees. Thin line of the incoming tide he walked along, toes curled in the faint wetness of a wave turning back. I feel some guilt as if there was someone here whose area I had gone into. He said, still looking at the wall. We emerged from the cave, shook the sand from our clothes. I had seaweed in my hair. You are very beautiful but like a legend, he said. She saw the curve of his back, the heavier parts she went towards. His arms stiff at his side. She heard the clock. Felt the distances. Distance of beach, sea, the cave. White line of sand. He must have met her by now, in the arms of his fiancee. I want to remember this happiness, he said, I want to remember . . .

Two men watched an eagle, a snake, from their vehicle parked on the road side. They raised their guns, but did not fire. We waved, they did not respond. I felt their guns pointed at us as we walked on down the trail. The guns went off then, distant, half a dozen shots. The shrieks of some animal. Perhaps the eagle. Wings spanned the dust, sand. Blood that quickly dried. Sounds of carrions approaching. Men, silent in fishing boats, lowered their lanterns. In snake form they moved further out.

That part of the island deserted we walked towards the fig trees, and sucked the insides of figs. The inside of her legs a fainter white. His eyes blue. A blueness changed to green, according to mood, the weather, the light changing. His head rested against her legs. It's as if madness is just another trip

—like death, he said softly, and took hold of my hands, played with the fingers, one by one, as he laughed. Suddenly the whole nature of comedy becomes very clear like laughter which is a personal thing, he said.

I had laughed as his tongue probed my ear. Breath sounding there. A shell held close. Do you think we take on each other's madness? She heard the falling of fruit, saw a melon wrapped in willow leaves. Slender wrists turned in the airless cell. How is consistency ever possible I have no sense at all who I was yesterday, he said, fingers traced the outline of my mouth, face.

I laughed as he poked at the clinging thing on the rock, plucked out eventually. Am I a creature of my imagination —it's like everything is possible and thinking again what everything means if I enter the body then there's questioning the value in order to preserve the integrity of that world. The shell picked up again, held close, crushed, released in fragments. I feel as if I'm beyond the world—it's in a room there's nowhere I couldn't go—windows are open, he said, looking at the wall. Thick walls below street level. I opened the shutters. Why are you so restless? He crouched in the middle of the room, stared at the light. Let's go out really it will be all right I feel o.k. I want to see the sea—the sea.

He held onto my arm along the corridor. Along the cliff. He climbed over the fence. You see I am on the edge—just one push or one step. Tips of gull wings rose from the surface of waves. His face contorted, he balanced on his toes near the cliff edge. Ah you can't take this flight with me this time. He pointed at the swollen lop sided moon that tipped the mountains. Do you think you know the dark part of me? I saw the eagle, feathers around, and blood. Parts of fish scattered on the shore. Prints of horses in dry tracks. Faint traces on stones. A coral he picked up many miles from the sea. Sea that now moved in movements I touched. Can you hear the sound of stars? He asked, his face pushed into grass, earth. I was not sure whether he laughed or cried. Strange crying of some creature moving swiftly in the shadows behind her. A long drawn out cry. Manoeuvres in the dark. Tearing of flesh, fur. Sound of something dragged over rocks.

We walked down to the beach, and sat against drift wood. I watched his cigarette light up a part of his swollen face. Track of light the moon made on the sea. Three hundred yards the beginning of that where she could lift both feet up and walk on water. Grains in wood his fingers traced, she entered. Land many oceans spilled into. The way landscapes entered a room. Rooms she went through, corridors. Doors she opened onto carpets that grew towards trees, branches through walls, windows. Soft green light she touched, and was touched by. The scuttling of a crab or some other sea creature passed between them, over the wood. Movement under sand. Shifting of sand in front, behind. Flying fish between waves, those that fell out of the sea, fell back. These she listened to. And the sound of insects

against screens. Is it raining then, he said. Somewhere in a funnel a white moth, he caught, held until it no longer fluttered, wing particles on his fingers, he picked off bit by bit. I feel there's a hole in me somewhere that's dripping something out little by little, he said, without looking up. His head against wood, hair part of the darkness. In the low dunes. A low tide she went towards, stripped and dived in. She came up and saw his hands move slowly over his whiteness, up over his less white skin. She dived again, felt the bodies of fish, small, large, slide near, pass over, under her.

I climbed out, up towards where he slept. A limpness I

wanted then to disturb. I lay the other side of the wood and waited. Moon on one side, the sun came up on the other, bringing the mountains into focus. They no longer moved with the night. A cool breeze came off the sea. We climbed up to the cliff and drove back to the city.

The hotel that seemed some other place, in another city. Where she was alone. Where she walked the spaces between furniture. Lay on the bed, looked at herself in different clothes, or naked. Touched. Picked up the telephone, put it down without giving the number. Moved from bed to window, from window to chair, from chair to bed. She emptied the ash tray, waited to empty it again. The continual murmur of voices behind walls, shrill, low. Foreign voices. Televisions, bedsprings, those she couldn't hear, and sounds from the one after waking up with someone she didn't recognise, couldn't remember. The night. Several nights before. Who forced himself into her, forced her body to move until she cried out. Then no longer. Just his shadow against hers, until the form of three covered the space between door and window, between his thrusts, breath, the air through shutters, later cooling the wetness. Air she lifted her face to, watched the cigarette smoke curl, drift up, along, out. Spirals, circles of blueness he thrust away, turned and buried his head between her legs. While she took the other in her mouth.

This is a small city there must be small places to walk in, he said, looking through the shutter slits, where his fingers tapped, slid along. She stretched across the bed, watched the spools of light on his back. I think we are still being watched. He stood back from the window. There's a man on the corner—been there all morning I think he must be a Government agent or security police—do you recognise him? The sunglasses unmistakable. I could not be certain. He did not have a beard. And yet the suit, yes. He dressed, said he

70

wouldn't be long. I watched them shake hands on the corner, saw them get into a car. Later the telephone went, kept ringing until I reached the lift.

She walked in a small park all afternoon. In narrow streets, past narrow buildings. She sat outside a cafe half the evening. A place reminding her of another, where she waited, keeping off flies, and men who sidled up, or sat staring from nearby tables. He kissed the nape of her neck, fastened the hook at the top of her dress. She heard the waves touch the edge of islands. Curve of river below. The water carried cartridges. Sound of many guns exploding across the sea.

I found a message at the hotel, and took a cab to the address. The shutters closed. It did not look like a Government building. She rang the bell several times. She walked three times round the block, and knew then she was being followed.

In the museum he sat beside her. You like classical art then? She nodded. His leg shifted away from hers, back again. And his fingers, dry flesh, bitten off around the square nails. Yellow. She felt them in the small room he brought her to. Kept her there until there was no sense of day, of night. A blinding flashlight on her face. No sense of who touched her, who she was stripped by, who woke her as soon as she tried to sleep.

Who beat her with sticks, whips on the soles of her feet. Odours. The current of air a hand brought or hair not quite touching her face. Body. The changing darkness around the light. For how long she hardly knew, and after a while did not question. Wanting a closer approach. Straining upwards for the touch of another's skin she only smelt. Gestures she moved with on a narrow bed. The wooden floor. Sounds. Street sounds she tried at first to place, follow, keep in mind.

Other noises in another room. A man on a similar bed. Many women. Women he knew and those he wanted to know. They bent over her. The stronger odour, perfume. Her hand felt something round, soft. Fingers guided across. Pressed. Her head sank back, legs raised.

The light manoeuvred over a stuffed pigeon. A broken vase with paper flowers, dust covered. A steel filing cabinet. Next to this the man sat, smiling through cigar smoke. Yellow fingers tapped his crossed over knee. Shiny trousers. A small greyish moustache, the under bristles he now and then licked. He continued smiling. She noticed the bed was fairly large. The man stood up. She saw a margin of water in some small town.

A carnival procession. She could not cross a certain street. Masked, robed figures, their sex not apparent, thronged the pavements, roads. Three gathered round her. A certain recognisable odour, then gone. Streamers twisted in her hair, around her ankles. The man close behind. He wore a mask. His hands gloved. She pushed further into a more dense crowd. Someone, whose face was a painted mask, led her into a small space between the procession and spectators. She thought a woman held her hand. Wrists, fingers, whiteness of skin between the paint. A glimpse of his shoes, made her look for the mouth. But he had gone. Her arms pinned, unable to move backwards or forwards. Sideways she bent a little, head raised for air. The procession passed out of the town. She moved with those in front, behind her. At the town edge she was able to walk freely and quickly. Back to the hotel.

He slept in an armchair. The television on, sound turned down. A cigarette smouldered in the ashtray. She opened the door again and slammed it. He jerked up, attempted to smile from a yawn. Tie straightened. Cigarette squeezed around.

72

Ear plugs fumbled for, taken out of his ears, put in their container. I've had dinner, he said, what about yourself? I lay on the bed, aware of the smile. His. My own then, a kind of smugness, held on to. Until he switched the television off, and passed by the bed, then I noticed the mark, a bite on his hand. Some bloody dog in the park thought it was friendly and then

His knuckles white stumps beyond her ankles. She drew her legs up, felt their smoothness, the smooth eiderdown under her, either side. Not bad food they have in this place —a good steak—looks as if it might rain later been hot these past two days hasn't it? He stood up, searched for a cigarette, tapped it on the case, his fingers. She watched his movements, every move he might make, wanted him to make. Exaggerated her own gestures. Tensions in neck, spine, legs. I saw his bald patch the light caught. Around the light three flies chased each other, settled, began again. She noted three teeth marks just below his knuckles. She listened to the slight hiss of his breath between sentences, coming from a distance she thought wider, which she pushed further from the bed, from the wall next to the bed. The chair spun round. His face, not unlike the face he had in sleep, mouth half open. Hands not idle. Nails made patterns in the cigarette tip. Lines and crosses. Patterns she saw as signs, omens beginning from her knees, spreading out. Grass patterns made from the short grass, where she had fallen. Pushed by the procession, a man in a painted mask, in some gardens outside the town.

A slight stain of dried blood. Mud on her dress, her hand covered. Colours on the man's face merged, yellow into black, black over red. She heard the slight breeze off the sea, trees through narrow buildings. A door slammed. His lips pale in the midst of running colour. Lips folded in upon themselves. A mark he left on the back of her neck, with teeth she never saw. Rockets and circles of coloured lights above the buildings, broke, fell into darkness. The sound of these as they landed on the concrete behind her.

Thud of a body. Two men stood either side, poked his body with their guns. One stubbed out a cigarette on his chest and stomach. They threw water over his face, until the paint marks grew fainter. His mouth closed. A drop of blood at the right corner. The men searched his clothes. One looked up at her and grinned. They were soon surrounded by an applauding crowd. By dogs who had left off eating the carcass of one of their own kind. Grass flattened now, the divided parts where legs had been. His hands shifted around in his pockets. Informers are suspected everywhere—some of those masked men—ah one can't move around in this country as before—it's changed—changing all the time—are you tired do you want to go down to the bar?

Clink of ice against glass. Floating there. Small parts of shadow on the table. Under his eyes. Nicotine stained teeth. Pale yellow flowers, paler green stems hiding the rest of his body from her. Until he bent forward, knocked his pipe on his shoe. Shoes covered in mud. A leaf fell off, imprinted in darker patterns of the carpet. Her fingers traced the design of her dress. Flowers. Circles. Triangles. The lower part of his body. Curvatures. The slightness. And heavier tones of skin. Wanting to take in his history while taking him in her mouth. The journey around. The rigidness. When nearing the edge of what had gone before, he drew her up. His body made small jerking movements, each contradicted the other, from muscle to muscle, limb to limb.

In the mirror, he had propped up at the end of the bed, she saw angles of her own body that surprised. Parts he and others had delighted in. He watched his movements, and her face as she watched her own. Shifting around she saw her

74

legs. His back. And later the cliff, parts had fallen in. Thud of rocks taken in by the sea. Larger ones left, those against trees, half way down. A position she remained in, watching clouds pass over, or rest on mountains. Sound of guns in forests, where birds flew out above the smoke. Peasants paused in fields, watched a plane. In doorways, they silently counted the tanks, trucks and marching feet.

On a clear day the island could be seen from the mainland. Around the island the water was mined. The plane hovered, packages fell out. Trail of the plane above the sea remained all afternoon. Imprint of her feet in sand she went back over several times, until the tide made this impossible. On a high bank she caressed a shell, her hair, thin tall grass in patches. A blade she twisted around her finger. As he manoeuvred from her, his body still jerked. She saw her face in the mirror. The expression unlike that she had thought he and others had not noticed afterwards.

Daylight first seen in the mirror, a slant of light through curtains, expanded in the glass at the foot of the bed. She sat up, did not recognise this face, changing, patterned with light and shade. Another person. Some other life. A time in her childhood. On a swing in large gardens, swinging into, out of light through trees. Some happiness. Had it ever happened. It was happening now. Then the terror, sensing it, knowing something was about to occur. A man. Her father. Brother. Some lover. He pushed the swing, the child swung high, through air, into space, higher. Her laughter. Cries of birds. Leaves burning in heaps on the edge of gardens. Smoke and sunlight. Hands, her own clutched the rope either side, under the larger hands. The man, smiling, knelt, took hold of her ankles. Moist fingers tightened. He pulled her off the swing.

I pushed the mirror back against the faded part of the wall-paper. He must be in the bathroom. Water splashing. Sliding of bodies. Contact of marble against her back. A stone wall studded with bullet holes. Area barricaded off, near the watchtower. He held his breath, head raised. Knuckles rubbed against each other, as he waited for the water to shoot out.

A hotspring pool below the mountains. Enough room for one. She lay on her back. He beside her on his belly. The tiny jet of hot water she arched her back under. Water trickled over hair, into hair. Eyes. Mouth. The only homosexual fantasies I ever have is like now with the sun, he said, touching himself. She placed her feet on rocks either side of the pool and felt herself warm, moist. Waterfall across the river, under the mountains, the only sound. Fish swept over, some flying, others struggled out of fast currents. She sat on a high rock, half naked, conscious of that nakedness, the clothed parts. Marks on her back, long thin red lines, and bruises. From a wooden floor. Narrow bed. A fall in some large gardens. His body unmarked, apart from the lines, crosses his underclothes had made. His fingers spread over himself, plucked quickly. Lightly along the lines on her back. She heard the hiss of the whip. In the mirror she saw him astride the girl. She struggled from the blows, but came back for the contact of leather against skin. Metal and water. Crystals raised. Under the waterfall, struggling next to uneven banks. Moving fast on top of mountains, in wider sections of the river.

He stood up, feet planted firmly on the rock. The bed. Bathroom floor. On the balcony she replaced articles. Wallet, cigarette case, several pens, pencils, notebooks, diary, cuff links, a tie pin. A list of names, those reported to have Communist records. A list she went through several times. He might have changed his name. She could not tell. What name would he have chosen. A foreign name. Spellings of proper names can vary. Another list gave those who had been interrogated, sentenced, given alternate doses of 'hard' and 'soft' treatment in cells measuring one metre by 1·90 by 1·20. A woman subjected to repeated electric shock treatment, now suffering from hallucinations and from continual trembling.

I was informed that no casualties had taken place in any detention camps. A photograph taken from the photo on the grave. Police were present at the burial—three or four of them—in uniform, the Minister said, taking back the photograph, sliding it into a file. This man the reports say while returning from the lavatory at five p.m. was shot twice in the left side by a black beretted second-lieutenant of the armoured corps he died instantly with a pierced lung—is there anything else you wish to know madam? I asked if we could meet the second-lieutenant in question, if he existed. The request to see the officer went unanswered. The interim verdict must be Missing, possibly shot dead while trying to escape.

I opened the folder of photographs. None of them bore any identity to each other, yet each had some singular aspect. A gesture. The stance of the body. Some showed only faces, faces in bad light, too much light. Out of focus. A ring on the middle finger of the left hand. Many such rings are made in this country, he said.

The island obscured by mist, though the top of the watch-tower could be seen. A rumour that detainees had been tortured. That the cells were infested with fleas, bugs and lice —deliberately put there. That prisoners are allowed out to the courtyard only for short periods twice a day. As soon as they fall asleep they are abruptly woken by guards and hurried to an officer's room for interrogation. A blinding flashlight shines in the prisoner's eyes throughout. This lasting for ten hours or more. Women are stripped naked for questioning. In between the sessions of questioning, the prisoners are not left alone. They are beaten with truncheons on the face and head in the cells, and are also taken to the terraced roof of the building for 'special treatment'. It was claimed that some have been interrogated at considerable length but had never been physically maltreated, because they were designated for appearance in court.

The buildings were empty. A peasant confirmed that there were no prisoners on the island. Today an itinerant vendor was sent for court martial accused of practising his trade without police permission and of selling tourists chocolate ice creams at excessive prices. Yesterday a farmer was sentenced three years for using insulting words against the authorities, he said I was born a democrat and prison is for the brave. In his defence he said he was drunk when committing the offence. A tailor, two years gaol for possessing a fully loaded revolver without a proper licence.

He was still in the bathroom. I searched the cupboards, pockets, lining. I knew he had a gun. It was unloaded. Telephone numbers on a scrap of paper. Names. Women. The address where the party had been held. A photograph, torn at the edges, of a naked girl gagged and bound, a look of pretended agony in her eyes. Another of a woman in black suspenders, boots, masturbating. A photo of myself against white railings, a look of fear in my eyes. I closed the cupboards, drawers. Briefcase. Brushed my hair as he entered. Ah I feel much better now—shall we eat out?

The restaurant packed. People spoke in low voices. Some hardly more than whispers. Waiters were noisy. Men hid themselves in, behind newspapers. Women looked at each other, gazed past, out of steamed windows. Mouths opened, shut. He lowered the paper. I recognised him at once. His fingers seemed more yellow. He did not appear to recognise me. When we got up, he asked for his bill. He was not in

78

uniform. There was some argument. The manager was called. We left quickly, and separated outside. I waited until the police arrived. They reappeared, the man struggled between them. In his defence he said that some rivals over a girl had informed on him.

I reached the hotel by a roundabout way. He was not there. During the afternoon the telephone went several times, I did not answer. When I tried phoning it had been cut off. The manager said all the phones were out of order, they would be dealt with as quickly as possible. I locked the door, stood by the windows. It was late evening. The streets were empty. Some tanks came slowly round the corner. I heard a train in the distance. A telephone ringing in some other room. Then steps along the corridor, paused outside. The door handle turned.

She sat in darkness that spread. Her fingers slid over the revolver. Pressed against her face. She flung herself over the bed. The cliff edge. Waterfall. A wave carried her nearer the island. Rocks pock marked. Some with bullet holes. The wall he collapsed against, blood spurted out of his mouth. His body still twitched. Hers she surrendered to, the spasms he manipulated. Afterwards his hand there, wanting to sense what it was like. Asking her to take his smallness in her mouth. The growth filled her. Legs round him, he carried her towards the mirror. Patches of dark hair merged. Separated, each smelling of the other. Narrow space in the middle of the bed.

Rigid she listened to the silence of the hotel. Streets. The city. Her own silence filled the room, swung her into sleep, dreams. Half awake, as he entered the room, opened a cupboard. Sound of metal against wood. A half dead fly in some corner. He sat in a chair facing her. She drew the eiderdown up to her neck. He closed the shutters, pulled the blinds down, paused, his profile caught by a passing car light that swung across, vanished, came back. A searchlight over his eyes, across her arms. She brought the blanket over. He passed her a cigarette, lit it, avoided her eyes. His hand scuttled across the eiderdown. The small pebbles between them. Sand harder where she lay, tufts of grass against her legs. Pile of bodies in a ditch. The burnt flesh. Remains swept up. Or left. Guns from the watchtower revolved under a flood of lights. Smell of rain, that slid across her face. Odour of tobacco from his jacket, something else she could not at first detect. A pungent smell. Maybe stale perfume mixed with dry seaweed the rain had soaked several times, left in days of dryness. Skin tasted of salt. Dry red parts of elbows. Behind the knees. Small parts she went back over several times. Larger areas she paused in. Pursued

into the cave, disturbing crabs, other creatures from green damp walls, greyish sand, a bed of black seaweed she fell into. Small seeds pressed into her back. Wet strands of hair covered bones she saw from a shaft of light thrown into the rock surround.

She stood between two sculptured winged man-headed lions. Doors padlocked behind her. Hall of marble and lime-stone slabs. A winged and human-headed bull, with a winged attendant in human form. Conquests and buildings recorded by inscription between the legs. Her hand shaped in the air a serpent supported by a tree trunk. She paused in front of a lion-headed fire goddess, another similar behind her. She read the inscriptions. Took note of signs. A horse's head from the chariot of Selene, goddess of the moon. As the moon sets, the four horses of her chariot sink below the horizon. The sun rising from the sea in his four-horse chariot, two horses of his team break the ripples. Her fingers and thumbs shaped the two hieroglyphic signs that always followed the name of a goddess, queen or princess. She sat in front of a centaur whose foreleg was raised against a headless man's penis. She followed a chariot race, seven horses, on a wall. Many of the horses' legs broken off. Looking round she noticed the room was empty apart from a keeper in the doorway who swung heavy keys.

Her heels clicked from room to room. Between two urns the man took notes. Aware of his heavier tread behind her. Beside her. Sound of wheels. Horses neighed as the procession passed by. She took her shoes off and ran through halls. Gardens. A fountain with mermaids spurted jets of water. A lion, the colour of clouds, against a cloudless sky.

A deserted street, with newspapers blowing from wall to wall, where advertisements peeled, red painted graffiti. Sounds of street vendors selling icecream round the corner. She walked towards. Balloons and candy, small statues of saints, the Virgin. She bought a postcard depicting one of the centaurs, careful to choose the one with the centaur's face looking less maniacal, which she stuck with sellotape on the wall above her bed. Next to a large artificial rose. A dried artichoke flower in an earthenware pot stood beside the bed, that fell off as he reached over to turn the radio on. In a suburb today a left-wing marble cutter lost most of his trade after police had cut off his telephone and warned his customers against patronising him. I think our phone is tapped—has been for several days now, he said, looking for a pair of scissors. Cutting up photographs of the woman. The girl. Photos in the park. Gardens. The spiral staircase. A car parked outside a government building. Many photos he had developed, redeveloped, blew up until faces merged with landscape, walls, rocks. Bubbles of the sea. A photo taken from the helicopter of the watchtower, no guns could be seen. Dark shapes that could have been faces at the windows. The shadow of the helicopter hovered over that of the tower, surrounding buildings. Many of these photographs he said

81

were blank. He did not cut up the negatives. She found them buried beneath a pile of clothes. She held each one up to the light, vague shapes, outlines occasionally that could have been faces, rocks, trees. Frozen forms. One she held up to the light again and again. A man, in profile, his hand held up, could be waving, or shielding himself. A warning. A gesture of welcome. She could not be sure. Only that this was unmistakably like her brother. She would have to get the negative printed. And then . . .

He came in, said they must leave at once. He flung clothes in cases. A cab was called. The negative would have to wait. She had waited long enough. Wanted to go on waiting. Await developments. He said he would go on ahead, she could follow soon after.

She went into a park, it was deserted. Trees made archways. Blue spaces. Wider green. Borders of flowers in sheltered areas. She ran up a path lined with poplars. She thought he must be there, near the bridge. Someone leaned over, leaned back, hand raised. She ran into a narrow green area. A playground, with swings, roundabouts creaking, moving slowly. She sat on a swing. And waited. City sounds, traffic in the distance. She could wait quietly here. Move with movements of the swing. Her own movements. He would catch the train to another place. Some other life. Looking for her from city to city. Perhaps. She brought out the negative, held it once more up to the slant of light through leaves. She tore it up until the black pieces fluttered down, around her, scattered with leaves under the swing.

I walked quickly through the park gates. Caught a cab. He was in the station waiting room. Ah good there you are —have you everything—I've got two singles no need for returns—are you feeling all right you look a bit pale? The train moved slowly in. Quickly out. Mountains, sea, valleys,

82

rivers passed across her face in the window. Good to be on the move again isn't it, he said, and took out his pipe, sank back in the seat, grinned across at her, patted her knee. Stockings with a trail of interwoven roses. Her hand covered the torn pieces of the negative in her pocket. She could piece it together. Maybe. There was plenty of time. Space widened out as the city was left behind. Small towns. Villages. Wide. Narrow rivers.

He took out a photograph, passed it to her. I looked at it several times. It was obviously the same one, he had printed just before leaving. I felt a slight ache between the eyes. Head spun from the passing landscape. Looks very like him doesn't it but it is a man born in this country—I made enquiries, he said, however there's the possibility that where we're going . . .

Another city. Some hotel. She would pace the rooms. He'd continue with his notes. She smiled across at him, and took hold of his hand. He placed her fingers against his lips. I saw her face in the window, in profile. Her hand came up, raised as if to strike out, but passed slowly across his head, through his hair, and swung further down, as the train halted on a high bank overlooking a vast stretch of sea.

September

Hotel room with large red roses on yellow wall-paper. Geography of dust behind air conditioner. Hard mattress, broken lamp switch. Curiously enough gives a sense of liberty.

City alive and austere. Green and yellow places to hide in. Be discovered against a bullet torn wall. Grape vines through cracks.

Leaving the harbour walking on air through the light

The women parading in early evening leave me with a pounding heart, a dry mouth and the awareness my trousers are too tight.

'You smell as though you've just risen from the ocean bed'.

He woke up covered in sweat. Clothes and sheet rumpled. He wandered around the room for a while, lit a cigarette and lay down again on top of the twisted rope of sheets. His mind numb, he looked at the creases in his trousers. Around him his day oozed out and over him.

A spider's web stirred by the wind against glass, against white curtains. It is her hair.

Sunday

Beware of the
demons. Hers
in particular

Living with a woman is one thing: the innumerable questions asked of one. Travelling with her is quite another thing: the answers expected.

He   Are you happy or unhappy?
She That's not a very important question
He   You live with such frenzied intensity
She Because there's nothing else to do—I would be eaten up by reality.

Curious to note how when she's talking my thoughts wander and because of this I hear many oblique sentences which escape others.

Sculptured faces I saw today were quite expressionless unlike their bodies.

Tuesday

Ashes and water

Stifling today. All the animals lie on their sides. People, trees, motionless. Women gossip on the terraces. Smell of coffee being roasted.

It is the climate they resist—this climate of tragedy.

85

Revelations I
don't believe in.
Remain lucid in
agony/ecstasy

The sun is very different here it tears through the body and eats out the heart.

A peasant woman's heavy laughter. It still rattles the almond branches, and in a few weeks' time . . .

He draws back from the sunlight as though someone were there pointing a gun—ah if only —but for a moment his hand rests on the window sill. Only for a moment.

In the hotel foyer the man who is still around. But it is a coincidence. Continue believing this.

The bullet had lodged in the man's right temple. His head rolled over. Drunk, terror-stricken his wife danced around his body.

The mind goes
out to meet
itself

A maniac in the cave I lie alone and look at the edges of the world.

Wednesday

Neither despair or delight under this sky and the shining suffocating heat continues pouring down.

From the Talmud:

A vineyard surrounded by a fence is not like a vineyard without a fence; but no man ought to make the fence more important than the thing fenced in. For if then the fence falls, he will tear down everything.

The shamir is a small crawling thing which cleaves large stones when it crawls over them. With its help Solomon built the Temple.

Friday

I ask of myself more than I can give. Useless to maintain the contrary.

You will dance on and look back at me, not count the scribbling foolishness that put wings on your heels, behind your ears.

Rhythm of windlasses and machines. Hulls of vessels lurched from side to side. In the chalky dust, sun and blood the man was carried swiftly away. Ah the taste of death and laughter in her dancing later.

Sunday

A black-figured vase painting: Europa seated on the bull passes in rapid flight over the sea, which is indicated by fishes and dolphins. In front of her flies a vulture, behind comes a winged figure holding two wreaths.

We have moved into another room, from here we can see the island quite clearly.

Feel your way through the room. To the bed. Drop your clothes on the floor and fumble for the pillow. Accustomed to touch she will not wake up. So the hours pass and not a move. The roof falls asleep and the street falls into a heap of metal.

87

A mirror gives a certain elasticity of attention which frees the mind for enjoyment of its special discretions.

In her nakedness she presents to him the surface of marble, which he slowly begins to cut other shapes from.

Sun and white houses leaves hardly any room for shades of meaning. However a mere smile on a woman's lips, a glance is enough.

Eat hands full of ashes, saints have lived on them. Are you better than a saint? Let the security police giggle to each other over their desks and use dirty towels in the lavatory.

Tuesday

Somewhere there seems to be a maladjustment.

Absurd	Form
Orig. deaf	formal
mute	formaldehyde
geography — earth + metron	formality
measure	formication
writing about earth	formidable
irrational	

Design from a
Krater: The
Sphinx is seated
88

He transforms himself into a satyr and goes in pursuit of a white skinned siren. He is gay,

on a sepulchral
tomb-mound. Two
Satyrs attack
the mound with
picks.

lustful, even so he turns back with a mocking
jibe.

Thursday

The harbour leaping with light. The dancers on
the quay.

The Centaurs used
to be cloud-demons.
They next became
mountain torrents,
the off-spring of
the cloud that
settles on the
mountain top.

He was tired. She said he was jealous. He
repeated he was very tired. Very well let me
stay on, she said. No you would only feel
abandoned. She was drunk and dizzy with
alcohol and music. Her feet and body, it
seemed, had no sense of gravity. He remained
rigid, pale amid shapes and shadows of columns
and people. Why don't you join in—ah you
and your middle-class Jewish upbringing—even
if you do get drunk you watch yourself never
a step out of place that's your trouble. Later,
much later, two days afterwards he forced her
body to dance under him.

Tuesday

A red figured
amphora :
Herakles lifts
his club to slay
the Ker of Old
Age who has no
wings.

Virile despair in the stelae today.

Hot face against the gun's cool metal. The
sound of the safety catch. He put his tongue
along the trigger, poked it in the barrel. Ah
what happiness, he said, watching this whole
performance in the mirror.

89

From a grave jar : The lid has been removed; out of it have escaped fluttering upward, two Keres, a third one is about to emerge, a fourth dives headlong back into the jar.

Two weeks in the city and we seem to be neither going forward or back. The papers carry the same goddamn news. Rumours make for excitement, despair for natives and exiles. There seems very little difference now between them, except the exiles seem able to get the money and clear out of the country more quickly. Threats, suspicion. Talk of detention camps. A university town with security problems. Growth of police power. Court martials. The regime, apparently has admitted in writing to the International Committee of Jurists that telephones are being cut off; the reason offered is that it prevents left-wing elements from plotting over the telephone. Relatives of political opponents are victimised. Very few people now allow themselves to get drunk.

'I'm not interested in the papers—it's the weather that troubles me if it will be a clear day tomorrow for our trip over the island', she said this evening.

A nail somewhere in the wall—a bullet perhaps—what has that to do with me. But a pin sticking in my shirt that's what pricks.

Relationships based on the master/slave situation. Roles reversed from day to day. As soon as one wakes up: the way the blankets have been taken over—the first one to get up—the role begins from there.

From a fragment
of an oinochoe:
a bearded monster
with wings, claws
and dog-like head.
She has lent her
orthodox lion-
body to Oedipus
who stands in front
of her.

The problem is to discover whether I can live
with this woman's demons without forfeiting
my own.

A painted screen that hides the scaffold from
him.

The wind from the mountain held us back, the
sea twisted from top to bottom. All sides. Above
the valley the cypresses flying. An eagle, the
only bird not flying from one mountain to the
next.

One great obsession gives an alibi for despair.
Remember this when next time she . . .

October

Sirens are running
naked in under-
ground caves.

What does waking up in this shuttered room
mean—sounds of the city—all is foreign. What
am I doing here, what is the point of this
laughter, these gestures, this woman whose legs
I part?

Admit I find everything strange and foreign.

She now used him
to perform her
own tragedy for
herself

She finds a metaphor for her condition without
defining it.

91

'It is my concern for happiness that causes me the most anguish'.

To make an order
out of myth/the
past

I would like to exhaust the limits of the possible.

According to Talmudic legend: forty-nine of the fifty gates were disclosed to Moses. What then lay behind the last one?

Thursday

Under the burning sun amongst the immense dunes the world narrows. But if a horse neighs, a dog barks, or the sound of a train in the distance, then everything, the dunes, sea, the sky fall into place, and then they lie at a vast distance from me.

October 3rd

Dream

A room opened out onto the balcony, its other door led into a second room. The only light came from the first which led to a third windowless room. Three women slept on a mattress, in an arc. Two of the women had large warts covering their bodies. The third a girl, whose face was very beautiful. I moved, crouched, fumbled in the room towards the girl. I schemed how I could get rid of her monstrous guardians. They woke up, though the girl continued to be apparently asleep. They rose and came towards me. I moved along the walls and could not find the door. The women caught hold of my arms, led me gently over to the girl. I felt their warts on their hands, they were small dead toads. Laughing the women disappeared. I fell on the girl and entered her, lay in her, grew large again inside her. She was utterly motionless, and yet I could feel her orgasms, several times, the heat, the flow. Overwhelmed by the sense of feeling her coming before me, and with me. Finally I got up and the two women appeared. It was then I noticed the girl was paralysed from the waist down as the women supported her across the room into the second one, and out on the balcony where she turned and smiled at me.

Have excess within limitation.

Wednesday

Is it her body I hold in my arms or the sea?

Line of hills and the chain of mountains behind the hills surrounding the bay. Almond trees along the road by the sea. Cypresses that are usually dark outlines against the sky, today this cypress streamed with light. Trails of light as the sun floods through a stained glass window.

He wore a mask no reason except to see things from behind a mask.

Rabbi S once said: "If I had the choice, I should rather not die. For in the coming world there are no Days of Awe, and what can the soul of man do without the Days of Judgement?".

If one could pick such and such a day to die how superior, how indifferent one would be.

However nowadays one cannot even choose how or where to die. Even that is taken out of our hands: to resuscitate or not to resuscitate.

Every debarkation an attack.

Saturday

Slow slow movements lifting over and under me. A distance from what has been preoccupying me. I walked along the cliff edge, feet holding the earth, the light around soft, sky so white. Then I knew I had experienced a kind of madness. Coming back to my body, a sense that I was perhaps someone else, some drifting thing that at least had found somewhere for inhabiting, not to remember happiness—just curiosity.

Madness: Flowers and bones. A face at the window. Someone singing.

'An ancient doctrine that the souls of men that come Here are from There and that they go There again and come to birth from the dead'.—Plato.

There has been a death recently no one has occupied the body since.

If going outside my body and I lose my ego what happens next? It no longer matters.

94

Monday

Her bird-feet trampled over my body as I began eating her wings.

Minerva's statue stripped bare of her clothes today, as is the custom: once a year.

He had forgotten the revolver was loaded. He played with the safety catch as usual. At last, he said, as he heard the gun go off inside his head.

A note on the door: Go Away I Have Shot Myself. They go away.

Wednesday

Primitive Greek mirrored his own human relations in the figures of his gods.

Afternoon spent with naked bodies, sunlight and hashish. She fell in love with her own sensuality.

The matriarchal goddesses reflect the life of women, not women the life of the goddesses.

When she saw him make love with another woman she became aware for the first time of his body, as a physical thing.

In the dark woods, on the moist earth, I found my way only by the whiteness of her neck.

The auricle of her ear felt fresh, cool. A shell to the touch on the tongue.

95

Hippolytus tore his brother Giulio's eyes out because the woman he loved preferred Giulio's eyes to Hippolytus's body.

I did not feel jealous until she asked me if I was.

Thursday

What if one loses all one's demons—surely new ones will leap in?

When Pentheus has imprisoned the Bacchus he finds not the beautiful stranger but a raging bull.

He shaped out of the wall a creature, a sort of half man, half woman. Just before he completed this the creature jumped out and began to unshape him bit by bit until only his toe remained, then the creature went out into the city and began . . .

A room caught between two others where others sleep.

Stretching his hands out over the bed he was surprised at not finding the wall. Imagine it, he thought, that creature I shaped must have eaten it up, and he went back to sleep.

AZAZEL: In biblical times, a mysterious desert creature to whom, on the Day of Atonement, a goat was sent "bearing the iniquities" of Israel. In post-biblical times this name was understood as applying to one of the fallen angels.

Cheiron always keeps his human feet and legs and often wears a decent cloak to mark his gentle civilised citizenship.

Saturday

Several new perceptions of the disintegrating creature that I am have dawned upon me consolingly.

96

View of the tower through mist: distracting.

'I can't leave the country because my mother is an old woman. She would want me to be at her funeral—after all it is her last great public appearance. She'd hate it if I didn't turn up for that performance'.

His father was a Hazan in the city synagogue, he died of a burst lung.

Prometheus gave Zeus two bags made of bull's hide, one contained the flesh, the other the bones. Zeus chose the bones.

His greatest obsession was to disappear—to go on a journey suddenly, without telling anyone, leaving no address. He could be found sitting outside a cafe before sunrise, delighting in the indifference of others as the weeks came and went. Soon he realised he would have to find another cafe. Another town. Some other city. Another room. And begin all over again.

What annoyed him most was her use of memory: yes it's just like that time when you. . . . or: it makes me sick because it reminds me of the time when you . . .

Monday

Something to be said for remaining in a place far off, without name, without identity.

97

The air is filled with screaming sirens.

The city is grey now. It was not always like this, he told her. They do not know whom to accuse. At night the cicadas make long flute-like noises, heard even above the rumble of machines, tanks. The smell of eucalyptus surrounds the city, penetrates the walls. It's the trees I don't trust those damned trees, she said, how can I feel compassion any more when even they are invading? She looked at him in distress, with madness in her eyes. But who is at fault?

A sudden fall of sand made the pebbles enter me and they summoned the sea. The sea.

Wednesday

The security police are everywhere, even in the carnival they mingled with those who were masked. I managed to get back to the hotel just before she returned. I cannot tell her that there's every evidence her brother is dead. The man showed me some photographs. He gave me a negative which I have yet to print.

The University town is enjoying this revolution. More tanks arriving in the city during the curfew. A few like myself watch through the shutters, others turn over restlessly in their sleep.

I had decided earlier today that this is a city we cannot remain in for much longer. But when she returned I felt I could not tell her.

She is convinced her brother is
on the island
shot through the head
taken another name
gone to another country
that he walks a deserted beach
a yard
a cell
parks
a museum

As long as she has a catalogue of places—a
file of photographs, addresses. Men who re-
semble, if only by a gesture, a hand raised, a
large ring on the middle finger.

She walks through narrow streets; enters dil-
apidated buildings, talks with Government
officials. Looks at a dozen or so men lined
against a wall. They all think her mad, but very
beautiful, untouchable except by those who say
they have information.

She was taken to a house on the outskirts of
the city. I had told the man to follow her, to
see that no harm came to her. I was in the
other room when I heard her voice. She sounded
angry. I pushed the two women away from me,
and went to where she was. The man said she
was asleep. I tried rousing her, but she fell back
moaning. I went back to the next room, the
two women were furiously making love, biting
each other, in a frenzy of limbs, licking each
other, their bodies making strange acrobatic
positions. I asked them if they liked being
whipped, they refused. They left and I heard

their laughter. Her laughter, I thought, or was she crying. The women breathed over her body, touched the air, two three inches away from her face, legs. She was smiling, but her eyes remained closed. The man read a newspaper.

I asked the women to leave, the younger one wanted to stay, the other didn't, they began quarrelling. We had to separate them, I still have the bite on my hand. The man said she would be o.k. he would see that she got back safely.

Friday

I can't even see the watchtower today, she said, standing by the window. I found her still there when I returned.

Saturday

Packages can be seen dropping from a helicopter onto the island, which means . . .

The clarity of all the events makes it mysterious.

The maggid of K said: "every day man shall go forth out of Egypt out of distress".

One of the things to do : exorcise. Exorcism, re-action in strength, in a bull-like attack, is the veritable escape for the prisoner.

From a vase:
a bearded man,
wearing a wreath,
reclines at a
banquet. A table
with cakes stands
by his couch.
An enormous coiled
snake is about to
drink out of the
wine cup. On the
reverse a woman
goddess holds a
sceptre, a girl
brings offerings—
an oinochoe, cakes,
a lighted taper.
Above are hung
votive offerings—
a hand, two legs.

I enter a thousand subterranean passages when I close my eyes.

I cannot leave you with this doubt, listen, she continued, I would never deceive you. She halted before the sea, and then plunged in. He waited for her to rise out—even a hand, some part of her, would have satisfied him. He continues waiting for some sign.

The sound of many birds in the trees. Their noise is deafening. The sharpening of their beaks against wood. But not one can be seen.

The hidden life of the skin. My intentions spring from that.

'I am born of too many mothers'.

Emerging from obsession which hasn't revenged itself yet, and which a hundred and one centuries of life would never satisfy now.

Branches luminous with blood on which no bird settles.

From a black-
figured olpe:
The slaying of
Medusa by Perseus.
Medusa has pro-
truding tusks and
tongue. Her lower
lip covered by a
fringe of hair.
Four snakes rise
from her head.
She wears a short
purple Chiton,
over which is a
stippled skin with
two snakes knotted
at the waist.
She has high
huntress-boots
and two pairs of
wings, one out-
spread, the other
recurved. She has
a bent knee that
indicates a striding
pace.

Dream

Medusa entered my room. I felt uneasy, certain
she only had evil intentions. I had the revolver
ready. I could just see her eyes, great glowing
ovals; I would aim at those—just two shots. I
knew she understood what I was up to. Her
eyes grew larger, filled the room. I felt their
heat. I fired two, three shots and the eyes fell
onto the floor, circled me, tried to rise like half
dead fireflies, then faded. I switched on the
light, her bloody head separated, rolled over
the bed, the sheets without even making a stain.
Then her head rose and fell upon me.

Cut-up dream

Medusa entered a room that opened out onto
the balcony. I had evil intentions. She had the
revolver ready. I saw three women, great glowing ovals, on a mattress, in an arc. I would aim
at those large warts covering their bodies. Just
two shots. I knew she understood the third,
a girl whose face, eyes grew larger. I moved,
crouched, filled the room with heat. The girl
schemed how I could get rid of her monstrous
guardians. They fired two shots, and the eyes
fell, though the girl continued to be apparently
asleep. The floor circled me, tried to rise and
come towards me. The walls like half dead
fireflies caught hold of my arms, led me gently

over to the girl. I switched on the light. I felt
the warts on their hands, her bloody head
separated, small dead toads. Laughing the
women rolled over the bed. I fell on the girl
and entered her, lay in her. Inside her she was
utterly motionless. Her orgasms several times
made a stain, the second one out on the balcony, where she turned and smiled, then her
head rose and fell.

Her neck was so oblong and delicate it could
have been sliced so thinly and evenly. He did
not fail to notice this immediately, it was very
tempting. He politely refused while thanking
her at the same time.

You must realise that I am another woman
by the evening. In that case, he said, I shall
only see you during the day.

November

I am constantly amazed by the strangeness of
natural things and the naturalness of strange
things.

A squadron of horses on a spiral staircase pre-
sented itself several times during the night and
by sunrise they came down; nothing absolutely
nothing could prevent them, nor the moving
stairs as I began climbing.

Ranks of powder-grey olives each throwing a long morning shadow across the damp grass. Pink asphodel spring from old grey stones, many-clustered flowers standing quite still in the warm windless air. Red and blue wild anemones crushed by marching feet.

The Siren invasion took place with regularity and sureness

Tuesday

When I leave this country will I look back on it with nostalgia—only the possibilities that were missed. Perhaps.

Her mood drove him out. Only when he was on the bus half way across the city did he realise that it had been his own mood she had not taken into account.

In his dreams he knocked her over, raped her, beat her until the blood covered them both, and finally he strangled her as he had the chickens for his mother at the age of twelve. So that he always expected her head to shake a little afterwards, and he'd wake up feeling cheated. Nevertheless the next time . . .

Vase painting from a cylix: Out of the ground rise two heads. Dionysus and Semele. The god holds aloft his high-handled wine-cup, behind him and Semele a great vine is growing, up one side clambers a Satyr.

Unlike most men he gave her no patterns to abide in, therefore she had to make her own patterns, because of this he felt himself caught up entirely with her rhythms. While she

Sometimes he is sad to see himself so restricted. He goes wild. He leaps over the furniture and begins to neigh, to neigh persistently and loudly in the hope that someone will come and leap on his back, spur him forward, if only into the next room.

The execution will take place this morning Prisoner have you anything more to say? Yes I'm sorry but I haven't been following this case but please allow me one more dream.

A dream can often make me fear death, as if when I wake up I taste and smell death there even in a cup of coffee. I refuse to be resigned to it, therefore fight it and that only leaves me exhausted, my body a tomb I neither enter or struggle out of.

I asked him to take off his mask, but this is all I have, he replied. Take it off I commanded. He did so. It's no use I still cannot recognise you—put the mask back on—there that's better now that I know I don't know you we can talk more easily.

A dog with a rotten tongue hesitates to eat the carcass.

Red-figured vase painting: a man-fronted monster

She cannot live without sensations. She will like some sorceress shape them out of air itself

105

body of a bull,
from his mouth
flows the water
of his own stream
Achelöns.
Herakles is about
to break off his
mighty horn;
Deianeina stands
by unmoved.

it seems and then present them as if they were the most natural events. But oh beware the man who accepts them as such, then she will carve out his mind and heart, leaving him to cope with the remains.

A fly washes itself and reminds me there is so little time.

He walked into the deserted park. It was late at night. He sat on the sloping bench, and began as usual to people the park, unpeople it, arrange, rearrange the trees, the lamps, until he had the setting just right for his usual plan of coming across a body, what he would do with it; this varied according to whether it was a woman or man. He had just arrived at the crucial point of turning ·the body over to see the face, when he was greatly disturbed by the sound of someone running down the hill. He waited until the man had passed him, then gave chase. At last, he thought, now I will find out what can be done, and how I might really feel—all the same I wish it were a woman I rather felt like coming across a woman's body tonight—ah well best to leave it for some other opportune moment.

There are spiders in three corners of the room. Leaves shake on the chair, which if touched I know soon enough will be the fibres of the chair. And the spiders—already they make their wall of webs across to the fourth corner of the room.

I wish to be alone then once I am alone I long for company. For once on my own I am confronted with those who inhabit me. I become a prisoner of my own imagination, more so now in this city with its narrow spaces. The traffic could be the sound of a heavy ocean. It is.

Citadels in the artichoke flower.

Steps
a tree,
porticos,
white stems
Setting for a murder.

On a Vapheio relief: A bull firmly meshed in a net, in another scene the animal has evaded the trap, throwing down one hunter who falls helplessly on his back, while a girl has locked her legs and arms around the monster's horns in such a way that it is impossible for him to transfix her.

Sunday

Aware of the distance, the length between hand and elbow. The bend of her neck as she brushes her hair. The light on the dust in the mirror. She brings her brother's presence in the sharp turn of her head. What can I do—continue being a metaphor for her despair?

She sketches out her dreams on his skin.

November 10th

All I ask is to be left in peace with my own madness.

107

A roomful of women a man enters. He feels as though he has suddenly, accidentally come upon a group of conspirators, hatching an assassination. No use their smiles, cheek kissing, cakes and drink offerings. He knows it will only take a false move on his part and the signal will be set off, then they will pounce on him, tear him to pieces. So he sits on the edge of a chair, surrounded by the smell of chocolates, almonds, gin and fur. Turning this way and that to the women, who sit back, adjusting their bodies in preparation, watching, listening to him, smelling his male smell of tobacco, leather and old crumbs in the pocket lining.

He concentrates on balancing his cup, plate, pipe and the lighter for a cigarette that suddenly is produced from a woman's jungle bag. He shifts from the edge, and the noise of the cup rattling, breaking around him comes as a sweet signal to his ears, followed by the wings beating against walls, the windows.

Wednesday

I face the mirror in my Jewish hair and ask why aren't you more of a Jew as befits one in exile?

How many hours I waste lying in bed thinking about getting up. I see myself get up, go out, move, drink, eat, smile, turn, pay attention, talk, go up, go down. I am absent from that part, yet participating at the same time. A voyeur in all senses, in my actions, non-actions. What a delight it might be actually to get up without thinking, and then when dressed look back and still see myself curled up fast asleep under the blankets.

Saturday

Days like this are taken up with nostalgia—longing for some other climate, another person, another love, until they are all spread out like a vast geographical map. There are so many routes, they all lead me finally to the edge of where I am at the moment: in a room I know only too well, a woman I love, but hardly know, and a city where every street declares its defeat.

It has come to the point when no one belongs to any one country least of all to oneself.

On discussing a picture:

Do you think he has just entered her?
Oh definitely
Which of them do you like best?
The woman of course
What do you think that snake is doing?
Is it perhaps jealous?
About to bite his toe?
Go up between them
Inside her as well

A voyeur
A pet
Look isn't it making love with itself
The man looks preoccupied
What do you think he is thinking?
I don't know but then the woman also looks
    off into space
Maybe he has seen the snake and not wishing
    to alarm the woman he's just entered he is
    planning the best way to kill the snake
Perhaps it is only a guardian
A spirit looking for a body to take over
Shall we try that position?
But there isn't a snake to join us.

Monday

A frescoe:
A girl acrobat
has hold the horns
of a bull at full
gallop, one of the
horns runs under
her left armpit.
She is about to
perform a back-
ward somersault
over the animal's
back. A second
female performer
behind stretches
out both her hands
as if to catch the
flying figure or
to steady her when
she comes to earth
the right way up.

Day after day I search for the girl. Ah yes and
then supposing I do eventually find her, what
then? Perhaps the orgy my imagination com-
poses is better than the actual thing? The bend
of her body under the whip, would I really
arrive at the same satisfaction a second time?
But a dozen times I go over it, half awake, in
dreams sometimes it is the other woman who
handles the whip, who dances over me, my
body covered in sperm, sweat and blood. And
in her mind, as we make love in front of the
mirror, what forms does she really see there?
I force her to dance under me, over me,
delighting in the swing of the hair like water
flowing backwards. The sweep of that over
me. Her laughter as the guns go off in the
distance.

Wednesday

She showed me a photograph of a child on a swing in some large gardens. That was the happiest time, she said, and everything began there.

December

I am on the verge of discovering my own demoniac possibilities and because of this I am conscious I am not alone within myself.

The question then: who is it today that inhabits me?

Metamorphosis

There must be time enough for preparation and for destruction, for the scheming, for reconstruction. A kind of dream made to order. To arrive finally at a unit with contradictory attributes never moulded or fused together, but clearly differentiated.

Tuesday

A distance now that never reaches its limits.

Friday

I am midway in the funnel—both ends I can see, one perhaps more clearly which I go to-

An ancient tribe of the Kouretes were sorcerers and magicians. They invented statuary and discovered metals, and they were amphibious and of strange varieties of shape, some like demons, some like men, some like fishes, some like serpents, and some had no hands, some no feet, some had webs between their fingers like geese. They were blue-eyed and black-tailed. They perished struck down by the thunder of Zeus or by the arrows of Apollo.

III

wards, then the funnel breaks in half. There's only the one way now to reach.

A new order of space.

So let us begin another journey. Change the setting. Everything is changing, the country, the climate. There is no compromise now. No country we can return to. She still has her obsession to follow through and her fantasies to live out. For myself there is less of an argument. I am for the moment committed to this moment. This train. The distance behind and ahead. And the sea that soon perhaps we will cross

LANNAN SELECTIONS

The Lannan Foundation, located in Santa Fe, New Mexico, is a family foundation whose funding focuses on special cultural projects and ideas which promote and protect cultural freedom, diversity, and creativity.

The literary aspect of Lannan's cultural program supports the creation and presentation of exceptional English-language literature and develops a wider audience for poetry, fiction, and nonfiction.

Since 1990, the Lannan Foundation has supported Dalkey Archive Press projects in a variety of ways, including monetary support for authors, audience development programs, and direct funding for the publication of the Press's books.

In the year 2000, the Lannan Selections Series was established to promote both organizations' commitment to the highest expressions of literary creativity. The Foundation supports the publication of this series of books each year, and works closely with the Press to ensure that these books will reach as many readers as possible and achieve a permanent place in literature. Authors whose works have been published as Lannan Selections include: Ishmael Reed, Stanley Elkin, Ann Quin, Nicholas Mosley, William Eastlake, and David Antin, among others.

SELECTED DALKEY ARCHIVE PAPERBACKS

PIERRE ALBERT-BIROT, *Grabinoulor.*
YUZ ALESHKOVSKY, *Kangaroo.*
FELIPE ALFAU, *Chromos.*
  Locos.
  Sentimental Songs.
ALAN ANSEN, *Contact Highs: Selected Poems 1957-1987.*
DAVID ANTIN, *Talking.*
DJUNA BARNES, *Ladies Almanack.*
  Ryder.
JOHN BARTH, *LETTERS.*
  Sabbatical.
ANDREI BITOV, *Pushkin House.*
ROGER BOYLAN, *Killoyle.*
CHRISTINE BROOKE-ROSE, *Amalgamemnon.*
BRIGID BROPHY, *In Transit.*
GERALD L. BRUNS,
  Modern Poetry and the Idea of Language.
GABRIELLE BURTON, *Heartbreak Hotel.*
MICHEL BUTOR,
  Portrait of the Artist as a Young Ape.
JULIETA CAMPOS, *The Fear of Losing Eurydice.*
ANNE CARSON, *Eros the Bittersweet.*
CAMILO JOSÉ CELA, *The Hive.*
LOUIS-FERDINAND CÉLINE, *Castle to Castle.*
  London Bridge.
  North.
  Rigadoon.
HUGO CHARTERIS, *The Tide Is Right.*
JEROME CHARYN, *The Tar Baby.*
MARC CHOLODENKO, *Mordechai Schamz.*
EMILY HOLMES COLEMAN, *The Shutter of Snow.*
ROBERT COOVER, *A Night at the Movies.*
STANLEY CRAWFORD, *Some Instructions to My Wife.*
ROBERT CREELEY, *Collected Prose.*
RENÉ CREVEL, *Putting My Foot in It.*
RALPH CUSACK, *Cadenza.*
SUSAN DAITCH, *L.C.*
  Storytown.
NIGEL DENNIS, *Cards of Identity.*
PETER DIMOCK,
  A Short Rhetoric for Leaving the Family.
COLEMAN DOWELL, *The Houses of Children.*
  Island People.
  Too Much Flesh and Jabez.
RIKKI DUCORNET, *The Complete Butcher's Tales.*
  The Fountains of Neptune.
  The Jade Cabinet.
  Phosphor in Dreamland.
  The Stain.
WILLIAM EASTLAKE, *The Bamboo Bed.*
  Castle Keep.
  Lyric of the Circle Heart.
STANLEY ELKIN, *Boswell: A Modern Comedy.*
  Criers and Kibitzers, Kibitzers and Criers.
  The Dick Gibson Show.

  The Franchiser.
  The MacGuffin.
  The Magic Kingdom.
  Mrs. Ted Bliss.
  The Rabbi of Lud.
  Van Gogh's Room at Arles.
ANNIE ERNAUX, *Cleaned Out.*
LAUREN FAIRBANKS, *Muzzle Thyself.*
  Sister Carrie.
LESLIE A. FIEDLER,
  Love and Death in the American Novel.
FORD MADOX FORD, *The March of Literature.*
JANICE GALLOWAY, *Foreign Parts.*
  The Trick Is to Keep Breathing.
WILLIAM H. GASS, *The Tunnel.*
  Willie Masters' Lonesome Wife.
ETIENNE GILSON, *The Arts of the Beautiful.*
  Forms and Substances in the Arts.
C. S. GISCOMBE, *Giscome Road.*
  Here.
KAREN ELIZABETH GORDON, *The Red Shoes.*
PATRICK GRAINVILLE, *The Cave of Heaven.*
HENRY GREEN, *Blindness.*
  Concluding.
  Doting.
  Nothing.
JIŘÍ GRUŠA, *The Questionnaire.*
JOHN HAWKES, *Whistlejacket.*
AIDAN HIGGINS, *Flotsam and Jetsam.*
ALDOUS HUXLEY, *Antic Hay.*
  Crome Yellow.
  Point Counter Point.
  Those Barren Leaves.
  Time Must Have a Stop.
GERT JONKE, *Geometric Regional Novel.*
DANILO KIŠ, *A Tomb for Boris Davidovich.*
TADEUSZ KONWICKI, *A Minor Apocalypse.*
  The Polish Complex.
ELAINE KRAF, *The Princess of 72nd Street.*
JIM KRUSOE, *Iceland.*
EWA KURYLUK, *Century 21.*
DEBORAH LEVY, *Billy and Girl.*
JOSÉ LEZAMA LIMA, *Paradiso.*
OSMAN LINS, *Avalovara.*
  The Queen of the Prisons of Greece.
ALF MAC LOCHLAINN, *The Corpus in the Library.*
  Out of Focus.
D. KEITH MANO, *Take Five.*
BEN MARCUS, *The Age of Wire and String.*
WALLACE MARKFIELD, *Teitlebaum's Window.*
  To an Early Grave.
DAVID MARKSON, *Reader's Block.*
  Springer's Progress.
  Wittgenstein's Mistress.
CAROLE MASO, *AVA.*

FOR A FULL LIST OF PUBLICATIONS, VISIT:
www.dalkeyarchive.com

SELECTED DALKEY ARCHIVE PAPERBACKS

FOR A FULL LIST OF PUBLICATIONS, VISIT:
www.dalkeyarchive.com